In the Silence of the Stone

Acknowledgments
I would like to thank my family
for their love, support, and encouragement for this project,
particularly: my husband, Todd,
who never fails to celebrate my creative pursuits;
my daughter and cheerleader, Arielle,
who is always ready to lend a hand
and whose detail orientation rivals the best
of professional editors';
and my sister, Kim,
who has been a source of linguistic
and literary inspiration my entire life
and without whom I would have never attempted
to write anything other than a shopping list.

ISBN: 978-1-68192-529-5
LCCN: 2019939966

Copyedited by Nancee Adams
Designed and built by Steve Nagel
Cover and interior illustrations by Susan A. Howard

PRINTED IN THE UNITED STATES OF AMERICA

MIST AND MERCY
BOOK 2

In the Silence of the Stone

by

Susan A. Howard

Our Sunday Visitor
Huntington, Indiana
www.osv.com

1
Hero of Mortinburg

The glow of the bonfire frolicked over their eerie faces. Like gargoyles, the bounty hunters chuckled at Waljan's fate. Their distorted orange faces fit the sinister mood of this chilly fall evening.

Waljan of the Realm, famed Knight of Abidan, felt more like Waljan of the Fools, Snared Rabbit. He'd been snared before. But since the Battle of Centennial Court, he'd ridden high on the gratitude of the citizens of Mortinburg, and things more often went his way.

The prickly rope chafed Waljan's wrists. Lashed to a rough pine, he struggled against the restraints. The knots only tightened. At least the numbing cold dulled his pain. As his captors rested and discussed his fate, Waljan thought, *Some hero I've turned out to be. I can lead a successful battle against corruption but can't free myself from a small band of half-wits!*

After expelling the manipulative Judge Asmodeus and his goons from the city of Mortinburg, Waljan had enjoyed his status as resident hero. At first, celebrity fit him like the boots of a much larger man. But he grew into it quickly—or so he thought. After all, it was celebrity and heroism that led him to his current dilemma. Now all he could do was sit, wait, and hope.

So he sat. He sat as he had for hours, studying his captors as they ate, laughed, and told tall tales. One particularly irksome fellow tossed around a smooth opalescent stone he'd taken from Waljan's pack. Mack, as his gang called him, recounted an old myth about Maweth, the Shadow Assassin. It was clear to Waljan that the man made up the entire story just to belittle him.

"Maweth, in his fury," Mack said with deliberate suspense, "conjured up the malevolence contained in his ghostly death stone."

"Oh for pity's sake, it's a *speaking stone*, you witless lump!" Waljan murmured as if arguing with his own flickering shadow.

The man continued, "Unseen, unheard, undetected, the malevolence seeped from the death stone and crept through the land. One by one, it turned Maweth's enemies to dust. With each offense, it gained strength, leaving no traces of the assassin's evil acts. Justice could never touch him. Until today, eh, lads?"

The men broke out in cheers and laughter. They taunted Waljan, "How's it feel, Maweth, to finally face justice? Ha!"

"I have told you," Waljan spewed. "I am Waljan of the Realm, Knight of Abidan. Free me now or suffer the wrath of the king!"

The men laughed all the louder as Mack shouted orders for more ale and rapped a tin cup against a rock. A boy of about twelve, hunched and nervous, came shuffling over with a jug and filled the men's empty cups.

With a quiver in his voice the boy asked, "Do you really think this is Maweth, the great assassin? He doesn't seem old enough to me."

"Shut your trap, boy!" Mack barked, aiming his fist clumsily toward the boy's head. With practiced reflexes, the boy dodged the blow, spilling the contents of his jug on the hot rocks that encircled the bonfire. The foamy liquid sputtered into a yeasty vapor and spiraled away with the breeze. "Now look what you did, whelp. No food for three days for wasting my ale!"

To Waljan's surprise, the boy took little offense. The boy knew that Mack would forget his threats by morning, as he often did. But Waljan didn't know that. The injustice of the boy's treatment enraged him.

"The boy did nothing to deserve that," Waljan scolded.

"Enough out of you!" Mack demanded in reply, hurling the speaking stone in Waljan's direction.

Waljan threw his head forward just in time. The stone ricocheted off the tree trunk, bounced off Waljan's shoulder, and plopped safely between his knees. Waljan trapped it and slumped forward as if knocked unconscious.

"What a shot!" came a chuckling voice from the direction of the bonfire.

"You think I nailed him?" Mack asked, amused.

"Well, whether you did or not," said a third voice, "it worked. He's quiet now."

"Yeah," Mack replied. "Let's get some sleep. We got a long road ahead of us in the morning."

The men knocked the burning logs about and emptied their cups over the fire. Spitting and hissing, the embers blackened and cooled. In the darkness, Waljan watched the shadowed figures roll out their bedding and blankets. He ached to be among them, warm and free to stretch his cramping muscles. But now, at least, he had hope of escape.

When deep, rumbling snores overtook his captors, Waljan gently shifted his legs back and forth until the stone beneath them began to glow. It was a long shot, but if he could contact the Realm and use the stone as a beacon, hope remained. The trick was to do so without alerting the bounty hunters. He tried to obscure the stone's light as best he could, but it escaped, streaming in all directions.

Shuffling and groans issued from the camp, but Waljan had to risk the light. He craned his neck toward the glow. He whispered, "My Glorious King, I need your help. I'm captured in Cloakwood, prevented from completing my mission. Please help me find a way out!" Then, with a painful twist, he kicked the stone as far as he could into the brush.

There was nothing left to do but hope. Wearily, Waljan slipped in and out of half-sleep. The steady, hypnotizing music of the forest at night seeped into his dreams, forcing him to relive bittersweet memories of simpler times. The freckled face of his dearest friend Penelope materialized and then dispersed like dandelion snow. As the image spun away, snarling jaws snapped, inches from Waljan's nose, and jerked him out of slumber. All in the camp was quiet but the pounding of his heart.

Waljan, you fool, he thought. *Still more afraid of your own sleep than the real trouble at hand.* The rush of adrenaline warmed him a little and cleared his mind. Falling back to sleep was unlikely, so Waljan decided to recite from the Edicts of Abidan. "Be strong and courageous, for the king walks ever before you. Wait on the king, for he is faithful. The true Knight of Abidan is patient, his deliverance assured."

He recited for what seemed like hours as he watched the stars shift and the moon glide toward the horizon. Suddenly, a creeping sensation caught his attention. A rustling in the brush drew his gaze toward the black expanse of trees. For a moment, he thought he saw movement. He listened. Nothing could be heard but the rolling call of an evening scrub grouse.

From the opposite side of camp, heavy footfalls followed groggy whimpers. "Why I gots to be the one to start the fire every morning? Thems always givin' me orders. 'Get up, Fenek.' 'Fetch the wood, Fenek.' 'Beat the prisoner, Fenek.' 'Make the grub, Fenek.' I just wanna sleep."

Waljan's confidence rose. He whispered sharply into the waning darkness. "Psst! Fenek!"

"What do you want, Phantom Assassin?"

"Why don't you let me start the fire for you? What good is a prisoner if you can't get him to do your work, eh?" Waljan suggested.

"How dumb d'ya think I am? If I untie you, you'll just murder me," Fenek replied.

"You? Scrawny *me* murder a big man like *you*? And without my death stone? Who knows where that landed after your friend hurled it at me."

Fenek giggled quietly. "Yeah, Mack's got good aim. Why would you wanna help me anyway?"

"To be honest, I don't. But I would do anything for some warmth. It's been a long night." The sunrise was still a good forty minutes away, and though the stars dimmed in the bluing sky, the forest remained dark. Only by the hesitance of Fenek's vague silhouette could Waljan anticipate the man's response. "Look," he pressed, "I am too numb and sore to cause you any grief."

Fenek stood there, taking moments to glance between the camp, the woods, and Waljan. Finally, as if forgetting why he arose in the first place, Fenek marched obediently over to the prisoner and untied his hands. Waljan slumped forward and rolled off the lumpy tree roots in agonizing relief. He suffered new pains by stretching out the old pains. But they were a better kind of ache. It was all so good until Fenek kicked him, hard.

"Well, get up! You gots a fire to build!" The man retrieved his blanket and sat in a satisfied bundle by the fire pit, waiting.

Between his palms, Waljan twisted a vertical stick vigorously into the notch of a larger one. Within minutes a line of smoke snaked out from where the sticks met. Blowing steadily, Waljan fed the heat until a ball of dried grass and small twigs burst into flame. Quickly and steadily, he picked up the fireball and placed it beneath a tower of logs. The flame wriggled up and grew into a welcome blaze. Waljan relished the fire with silent gratitude. He closed his eyes and let the heat ease into his bones.

"You make a pretty good fire, Assassin," Fenek admitted, snuggled up and completely content. His comfort lasted mere moments.

Chaos erupted from the dark forest. A low, snarling figure bounded past Waljan, cleared the growing bonfire in a furious leap, and tackled a screaming Fenek. Tripping over their bedding, the blurry-eyed bounty hunters scrambled to their feet. They groped for their weapons in the dim light, hindered by prickly pinecones and spiteful stones. As the sun crested over

Penelope sighed. "How about I just shoot you instead?"

"Okay, you lovebirds, knock it off!" Penelope's brother, Culbert, scolded. "Can we take anything seriously with you two around?"

"I think she sounds more like a crow than a lovebird, Cully, don't you think?" Waljan quipped one last time before finishing up the knot around Fenek's wrists and ankles.

"Wally!" Cully insisted.

"Okay, okay," Wally laughed. "Now . . . where is that kid?"

"What kid?" Cully asked, scanning the camp.

"There was a kid . . . he must be hiding somewhere."

"You leave my little brother alone!" Mack demanded. "He didn't do anything to you."

"Your *brother*?" Waljan asked, his eyes narrowing. "Hey, kid! I'm not going to hurt you. Come out." Waljan listened intently. Hearing no movement, he continued, "You're a pretty smart kid, you know? You were right the whole time. I'm not the assassin. Come on out. I have an offer to make you."

"Don't listen to him, Ander!" Mack demanded.

Waljan crouched down and spoke directly in Mack's ear, "Here's the thing. I should leave you all here to rot for the way you've treated this kid—your brother, no less. But I'm thinking he may—*may*—object to that. Things will go far better for you if you just settle down and let me talk to him."

Mack considered his words. Realizing he had no other choice, he yelled out to his brother. "Hey, Ander. It's okay. I think the assassin is going to let us go. Come on out."

Everyone focused their attention on the perimeter of the camp. A slight rustle sounded from the forest. Pausing a moment while gesturing for all to remain still, Penelope glided soundlessly toward the rustling. After a moment or two, she reappeared, leading the frightened boy to Waljan's side. With eyes averted, the youth seemed as though he might collapse into himself and disappear.

"There. Now, look. Everyone is fine, you see?" Waljan said warmly. The boy nodded. "It's Ander, right?" The boy nodded comfort. The travelers climbed out of Cloakwood Forest into the foothills that connected Mount Sar to Shroud Peak. In all Mortania, the Crescent mountain range held the most beautiful landscapes.

With Bo Dog at their heels, Penelope and Ander walked together, ahead of Waljan and Culbert. Penelope had a way with most people and managed to secure the boy's trust. Waljan often said that when she had the mind to, Peep could charm the sass out of a badger. He assumed it was her feminine side or maybe the influence of her late mother.

"Why does he call you *Peep*?" the boy asked Penelope.

She smiled. "It's just a nickname. He's always called me that. We grew up together. He probably had trouble pronouncing *Penelope* when we were little, and *Peep* just stuck."

"It must be nice having lifelong friends," Ander said.

"Well, a good friend doesn't have to be one you've known forever," she replied.

"I wouldn't know," Ander said with a sad smile.

"Are you going to be okay going back to your brother?" Peep prodded.

"Mack's my half brother. And he's not so bad, really," said Ander. "He's got a temper. But he means well."

"Well, that's not the impression Wally got," she replied.

"It's just . . . they really like their ale, and it makes them kinda cranky. They don't even realize it; they forget it all by morning. It's a rough life, bounty hunting. Always on the go, never settled down. Hunting, delivering, collecting money and then starting all over again. And it's dangerous. But it keeps us all fed, you know?"

"Where are your parents?"

"I never knew Pops. He was an adventurer. Went off to seek his fortune and never came back. Mack says the day I was born, Pops took one look at me and he was gone."

"That's an awful thing for Mack to say!" Peep said.

"He's only joking. Although, he misses Pops a lot and I think

"That's not nonsense. It's true. Although I have never seen a death stone like yours."

"Uh-huh. Because it's not a death stone. There are no death stones. This"—Waljan held up the stone for emphasis—"is a speaking stone. We use it for communication. It's harmless."

Ander looked as if Waljan had just told him that up was in fact down or that water was dry.

Waljan continued, "In any case, I am thankful you found it. I completely forgot it wasn't in my pack. You're lucky Cully and Peep didn't trip over *you* out there in the brush. That probably wouldn't have ended well."

"We should keep moving, Wally," Culbert suggested. "Gonna be dark soon."

Waljan found a stump and sat. "First things first. Moriel and Haden need to know where I am." He gently rolled the stone around in his palms. Nothing happened. The surface remained opaque and unlit. After a moment of puzzlement, Waljan tensed up. "Something's wrong. We have to get going!" he said, sprinting off in a new direction.

Culbert and Penelope exchanged confused glances. "But Wally!" Cully shouted. "That's not the way back to Mortinburg!"

"We're not going back to Mortinburg!" Waljan yelled back. "Come on!"

2
Shards and Sages

"No, no, no. Oh please, no," Waljan groaned as he plodded into the small village and dropped to his knees. He and his friends had traveled long into the night. But with a thick layer of clouds shrouding the moon and stars, they had stopped until daybreak. Now midmorning, the travelers arrived too late to prevent the tragedy that visited before them.

Coming up behind Waljan, Penelope nocked an arrow instinctively and scanned the smoldering ruins. Several outbuildings had been incinerated, and the orchards and vineyards had been reduced to rows of sooty sticks. A putrid haze hung in the air. Serenaded by the crackling gasps of dying flames, Cully searched the debris.

"Wally," Cully said, "There are bones here. We should look for survivors, just in case." Waljan remained in a slump. "Come on, Wally, get up," Culbert gently urged. Waljan rose to his feet as if he were lifting the entire world.

"How did you know?" Peep muttered.

Ander laid his hand on her shoulder. "I'm very sorry, Peep. Do you know this village?"

She lowered her bow, gazing at the destruction. "No, Ander, I've never been here before." She looked about her and then followed Culbert and Waljan. "We should help. Stay close."

A ring of tiny cabins remained standing among the destruction. Their contents—blankets, books, clothing, and tools—were strewn about. Ander picked up one of the books. The words *Songs of the Sages* adorned the cover with skillfully inked floral motifs.

A leaf slipped out of the book and flitted to the ground. Ander picked up the loose sheet and examined it. He folded it gently and purposefully and buried it in the pocket of his work apron, which he still wore from the previous day. Then he followed Penelope as she split off from the men.

In the center of the grounds, the shell of a longhouse beckoned, its door rocking back and forth on stressed hinges. Penelope and Ander peeked in cautiously. Rows of windows on either side dimly lit a swirling haze. Remnants of the collapsed roof still smoked. From underneath its beams, curious bits of sparkling light poked out in faint pastel rainbows.

"Hello?" Peep said. No response came. "No one here. Let's keep looking."

Penelope and Ander started searching the cabins from one end of the row as Waljan and Cully searched from the other. Each cabin was identical in its shape, size, and windowless austerity. Inside, a wooden plank, about six feet wide, jutted from the wall. It rested on two wide legs at the ends, forming a hard cot. In the corner, a slice of tree trunk served as a table. Emptied shelves ran along one wall.

The sameness and simplicity of each cabin were odd. Ander realized that this place could not have been a village, at least not like any he'd ever seen before. Not only was the layout and design too specific, there were no signs of children nor the hospitality of home.

Penelope and Ander finally reached the cabin where Waljan and Cully attended an elderly man. Distraught but seemingly unharmed, the old man sat on the edge of his cot, wrapped in linen like a fragile porcelain doll. A shock of white hair coiled at the top of his head. In folds, skin draped over his thin skull like you Peep when you have such a beautiful name to match that smile?" Master Chen asked.

Penelope flushed. "I prefer Master Chenaniah, as well. Rest. I will prepare some broth."

The longhouse was the most prominent structure in the campus. Still, Ander led the men to it as if they would have had trouble finding it otherwise. Cully followed Ander through the threshold and waded through the shambles. Careful to avoid hot spots, he tossed blackened bits of the collapsed roof aside, making a path toward the center of the room. Through the ash, fragments of the Stone of Sages gleamed.

"Wally," Cully said, "these shards look like the same material as your speaking stone." Cully tried to piece the shards back together to determine the object's original shape. But every time he reached for a section of the splintered stone, shocks of pain shot through his hand and up his arm. "Ander, see if you can find a rag or something. These are sharp."

Ander backed up against the wall. "I wouldn't mess with that if I were you!" he said with a shudder.

Cully seemed not to hear him. "It must have been rather larger than your stone, though." Getting no response, Cully turned around. "Wally?"

Waljan remained by the door, gazing with anguish at nothing in particular.

"Wally? You okay?"

"Can't you see them, Cully?" he replied, haunted. "Can't you see them?"

Cully scanned the room as Ander looked on in confusion. "See who?"

"They're all staring at me, Cully. Weeping. They're weeping!"

"Who? Wally, I don't understand. What do you see?"

Waljan rubbed his eyes and broke away from the vision. "Never mind. I'm fine." He struggled to gain control over his trembling hands, pulled a cloth from his bag, and tossed it over to Cully. "We can't leave the remains of the Stone of Sages here.

We have to take them to Moriel. He'll know what to do with them. Ander, can you help collect these?" Wide-eyed, Ander stood his ground. Waljan was too busy giving instructions to notice. "We need every last piece tied up in this cloth. I am going to go speak with Master Chen and see if we can locate the rest of the council."

"The council?" Cully asked. "What is this place, Wally?"

"This is Miqodesh, the Sanctuary of Sages, home of the Agasti. They are elders of the elders. They maintain the portal between Mortania and Abidan through the Stone of Sages. Or did until now. We have to find the other Agasti," Waljan demanded.

"You heard Chen. He said they climbed Castle Wall. They're dead."

"We don't know that. I'm not sure he knows that."

"But, the bones . . ."

Waljan erupted, "I said we don't know that! You don't understand anything about this place. Let's just get these shards picked up."

"Okay, Wally. I get it," Cully said in a disapproving yet understanding tone. "Come on, Ander." Cully silently attended to the shards as Ander looked on. After aimlessly searching the ground, Waljan backed out of the longhouse, slowly and thoughtfully. Cully pulled off his tunic and wrapped it around his hand. "Well, come on, Ander. Aren't you going to help?"

"I don't care what Wally says. I have seen death stones before and I don't think you should be touching those." Ander slipped quickly out the door, leaving Culbert to finish the task alone.

Waljan trudged toward Master Chen's hut. Penelope met him halfway.

"He's sleeping now," she said.

"Now? *Now?* I need to talk to him! The Sanctuary has been defiled, the Stone is shattered, the Agasti are missing, or worse, dead and . . ."

"Wally! Listen to yourself. The poor man is traumatized.

Look what he's been through! Of course he's sleeping."

"But we don't have time for that! We need to find out who did this and why. This is not just an attack on a small village. It's an attack on the entire Realm. I don't think you appreciate the seriousness of what's happened here!" Waljan said with urgency.

"What do you want to do—prop his eyes open with sticks and interrogate him like a prisoner? Aren't these Agasti supposed to be given respect, especially by Knights of the Realm? What's wrong with you?"

"Well, what do you *think* is wrong with me?" Waljan yelled frantically, startling Penelope. He folded his arms as if to hold himself together. Shifting his feet back and forth, he rocked himself into a pace.

"Wally . . . you need to calm down. I have never seen you like this," Peep said, deeply concerned.

"This is all my fault, Peep. Eleven of the wisest men in Mortania are dead and it's *my fault*! I should have been here," he said, forcing the words through his cramping throat. "I should have been here, Peep." He gazed into Penelope's large eyes, longing to plunge into the well of empathy they had always been for him. Instead, he fell into a bracing pool of practicality.

"You should have been here to die with the others?" Penelope asked pointedly.

"I shouldn't have expected you to understand," Waljan huffed and stomped away.

As evening fell, everyone but Master Chen, who still slept off his trauma, sat uneasily around a bonfire. Ander poked the embers and obsessively tossed random bits of debris into the flame. He watched each piece blacken and squiggle in turn. Cully and Penelope sharpened their weapons and prepared their packs for the next leg of their journey. Occasionally, they glanced over at Waljan. He sat alone with Bo Dog's head in his lap, staring vacantly into the fire and stroking the dog's ears.

"So now what do we do?" she asked her brother.

"Well, I suppose we have to take Master Chen to a place he

can be looked after. There are a couple of towns within a day's hike that have communities we can rely on for help. Wally would know better than me, but the Abidanian Elders are going to need to be notified. That stone is a big deal to them."

"What do you think did happen here, Cully? And why?" she asked.

"It was Maweth," Ander interrupted without looking up from the fire. "My brothers have been hunting him. They thought they'd caught him. But obviously they had the wrong man."

"Man?" Cully asked. "Maweth's not a man at all. He's more like . . . well . . . a phantom, I guess. An evil. It isn't something you can catch."

"It isn't anything!" Peep interrupted in exasperation, scolding her brother with scrunched brows. "It's a ghost story."

"Oh, no. I have seen what the Shadow . . ." Ander's voice trailed off somberly. "Oh, never mind. It's just—he's real, okay? And dangerous. And so is that death stone Wally carries around—whether he knows it or not." Ander added gravely, "Whoever lived here . . . you're not going to find them, you know?"

"Yeah, we know, Ander," Cully said, placing a brotherly grip on the boy's shoulder.

"Well," Peep said, "we need to get Chen out of here, that's certain. But he won't be able to keep up with us. We need to make some means of transporting him."

"That's not a problem," Cully answered. "I'll build something at dawn tomorrow. We'll be able to get out pretty early. Why don't you see what Wally has to say about it?"

As Penelope approached Waljan, Bo Dog wagged his tail lazily. "Hey there, Bo. How's my pup, huh?"

Bo looked up at Penelope, his tail beating the ground. Peep scratched him behind the ears and snuggled her face into his bristly muzzle. Then she plopped down next to Wally.

"You knew," Penelope said. "You took out the stone and then you knew. How?"

After a long pause, Waljan answered. "A speaking stone is

made from a rare opal that has unusual characteristics. No one really knows how it works. But the stones work together. When they're cut to a precise shape, energy is amplified through them. The stones can be used to send and receive information on the energy waves that pass between them. Of all the speaking stones in existence, the Stone of Sages was the largest and most perfectly cut. It was so powerful that it could network all other stones together. I knew something was wrong when my stone went dark. That has never happened before."

"That's all? Your stone went dark? And then you knew the Sanctuary was in danger?"

"Well, there is a little more to it, but essentially, yes," Waljan replied.

"You okay?" she asked. Waljan stared into the black distance. "Look, Wally, I know this must be really hard for you. And you're right. I don't really understand it, not being Abidanian myself. But you can't take the blame for it. You are one knight against an unknown enemy.

"Master Chen seems like a very sweet old man and I imagine the rest of the Agasti were really special people. But we need to put mourning aside and make some decisions. Master Chen can't stay here alone. He needs medical attention. And people need to know what happened. Cully is going to make some kind of transport so we can carry Chen to safety. Do you know where that might be?"

Wally nodded and took a breath. "Dead Springs. You asked me what I was doing out here. Well, I was sent here from Mortinburg with a request for the Agasti. There is a lot of conflict within the Abidanian community. As we grow in number, it seems harder to navigate the competition among our elders. Too many want to speak for the king rather than serve him. It leads to a lot of confusion about what's true, what's expected of us, and how to behave. Those who are most loyal agreed that we should bring our concerns to the Council of Miqodesh—Master Chenaniah and the Agasti—to be sure we establish and follow the king's wishes, not our own.

"After meeting with them, I was supposed to rendezvous with Moriel and Haden at Dead Springs. That would have been a week ago. They're probably still there and very anxious for a report. I would have preferred to contact them by now. But those bounty hunters took my speaking stone, and now that I have it back, it's useless."

Wally rubbed his face slowly with both hands and exhaled. "How did you find me, anyway? What were you and Cully doing so far south?"

"Looking for you, of course. Everyone was expecting to see you at the Harvest Festival. When you didn't show, Cully and I weren't the only ones worried."

"So, not only did I fail to protect the Sanctuary, I ruined the Harvest Festival, too? I couldn't possibly have something better to do than show off my fletching skills to the adoring public?"

"Wally, you're being overly sensitive."

"I have reason to be. It seems like expectations are set too high. No matter what I do, people are disappointed in me."

"I didn't say we were disappointed. The people of Mortinburg appreciate you, and your community relies on you, that's all."

"Maybe I don't want to be relied on. Maybe relying on me is a mistake. It wasn't very long ago that I was happily unknown, free from the judgments of every last person in town."

"You are seeing everything upside down."

"I'm sorry, Peep. I'm going on days with very little sleep and the lack of it doesn't help in coping with this horror."

"I understand. Anyway, everyone was worried about you, so Chaz Myrtle sent us to Cloakwood. Then, we tracked you from there. Honestly, we wouldn't have found you at all without Bo Dog. Isn't that right, pups?"

Bo grunted and rolled on his back for a tummy rub. Wally obliged.

"Okay," he said. "You and Cully have a good plan. We'll head for Dead Springs in the morning. Right after I get a thorough report from Master Chenaniah."

"And what about Ander?" Peep said.

"What about him?"

"Wally. You told Ander he could return to free his brothers and the bounty hunters."

"Oh! I completely forgot about that. But does he want to?" Wally asked.

Peep raised her eyebrows. "Are you really asking that?"

"Well, I wouldn't want to. In any case, we can't send him back alone, and I need all of us to help with Master Chen. I doubt Chen weighs much, but with our packs and gear I can't spare anyone. Ander has to come with us to Dead Springs, and from there we can send him to Cloakwood on horseback. His brother's gang is a tough bunch. They'll be okay."

"Wally! It will take us a week, maybe longer just to get to Dead Springs under these circumstances!"

"It's not like we have a lot of choice, Peep. It's the survival of the last of the Abidanian Agasti—and a witness to an egregious crime—against the inconvenience and discomfort of a band of questionable characters. Not a hard decision for me."

"Do you think it would be a hard decision for Ander?" Peep challenged.

"Do you have any idea what kind of treatment that kid endured, Peep? Trust me, he's a lot better off with us. I can sleep with myself knowing that I am protecting him from those so-called brothers. Maybe he'll have a better future with us than with them."

"That's not your decision to make."

"And you think he's old enough to make the decision himself? Look, I didn't say I wasn't going to let him return. I'm just saying that for now it's best for everyone that he come with us to Dead Springs. This wouldn't even be an issue if his brothers hadn't ambushed me in the first place!"

"Fine—have it your way. Cully and I will trade watches

tonight."

"It's not *my* way—it is just how things are," Wally insisted as Penelope made her way back to Cully.

3

Cloakwood

"We should be out there searching, not sitting here like brooding hens!" Haden huffed, triggering a fit of coughing and sputtering. He sat in a corner table at the Dead Springs Tavern and Inn with his good friend Moriel and rancher Chaz Myrtle. The inn and town were appropriately named; the three men had been the only patrons all morning.

Chaz offered the old hunter a handkerchief. "Haden, are you sure you're all right?"

"Of . . ." He stopped midstream to clear his throat. "Of course I am! A few white hairs and next thing you know, everyone is trying to feed me prune mush and help me into a rocking chair! I may be old, but I'm not dead."

Sir Moriel, a leading figure in the Abidanian community, couldn't help but smile at his gruff friend. His mild amusement hid a deep concern for Haden's excitability. As a Knight of the Realm, Sir Moriel was used to a life of self-denial and hardship. But Haden was a layman. And even though he was experienced in the wilderness, he had aged noticeably over the past couple of years.

Moriel wished his old friend would take up less active interests than traveling Mortania in support of the Abidanian Realm. "Even the youngest and strongest among us need to rest some time, Haden. Chaz is right in his concern."

"Not with Waljan out there, lost somewhere in Cloakwood! If you two children don't want to come with me, fine. I can search the woods well enough alone."

"Haden," Chaz reminded him, "Cully, Penelope, and the dog are out there already. Wally is in good hands. You really shouldn't get yourself all upset."

"Shouldn't I? Why did we send him alone?"

"You know why we sent him alone, Haden. It's part of his journey. He is not a child any longer. He's a Knight of the Realm who must complete his Tribulation."

The Tribulation visited every young knight loyal to the King of Abidan. Waljan's formation in the ways of the king had been rushed and he was knighted earlier than most. There had been discussion among the Twelve—the community's council of elders—that Waljan was not truly ready for knighthood. Moriel disagreed.

"You knights and your self-punishment. Isn't life hard enough without you searching for misery?" Haden complained.

Moriel laughed gently. "He is going to be fine, Haden. Trust me. Now, let's order some breakfast before they throw us out."

A gust of wind rushed upon the three men as the tavern door swung forcefully open. Haden turned, hoping to greet Waljan. Catching sight of a tall and lanky young man, he turned back around in disappointment and took a swig of coffee.

"Well, Tyre Pruitt! You're a long way from home," said Chaz.

Tyre, son of the beleaguered widow Josephine Pruitt, had grown into a ruddy and responsible young man and was one of Waljan's close friends.

"We were just about to order some food, son. Are you hungry?" Moriel asked.

"No, sir, thank you. I ate hours ago. You gentlemen are getting a late start this morning."

"We don't have much appetite really," said Haden.

"I have news that won't help, unfortunately."

"Why? What's happened?" Haden asked.

"There's been an attack on Smithtown with many casualties."

"Anyone we know, Tyre?" Chaz asked.

"Can't be sure, Mr. Myrtle. Reports are sketchy."

"We'll organize volunteers and supplies to help," said Moriel. "Haden and I can't seem to raise a glow on our stones. Can you take a message back to Mortinburg?"

"Yes, sir," Tyre responded without hesitation. Then, reluctantly he added, "but there's more. Word throughout the region is that this attack is the work of Maweth, the Shadow Assassin."

Moriel froze, but Haden erupted in typical fashion, "What nonsense! Who came up with that cocka"—*cough*—"that cockamamie"—*cough, cough*—"suggestion?" he gulped down his coffee and cleared his throat hard.

Bracing himself for the answer, Moriel asked Tyre, "What makes them think that, son?"

"It was done at night, sir. They woke to an inferno in multiple locations."

"Well that just suggests the fires were set. Not only is Maweth long dead, but he was an assassin—a master swordsman—not an arsonist."

"It's the mysterious nature of it, I guess," Tyre explained. "No one saw a thing or heard a sound. It was completely random with no explanation."

"I see," said Moriel. "Fairy tales have legs in the absence of a logical explanation. A proper investigation will dispel that rumor."

Tyre didn't budge. He just stood like a statue, staring at Moriel.

"What, Tyre? Is there something else?" Moriel asked.

"Yes, sir. They are blaming us for this tragedy. They claim Maweth is somehow connected to the Abidan community."

It didn't matter that in day-to-day life the Abidanian community integrated seamlessly into society, whether in Mortinburg, Smithtown, Echo Canyon, or any other city. It didn't matter that citizens from among their community were typically hardworking and law-abiding. Nor did it matter that Abidanians often took the lead in improving the living conditions and safety of the cities in which they lived. As members of a community that professed loyalty to the king of another land, they were regarded suspiciously, despite their deeds. And although Abidanians had enjoyed greater acceptance in Mortanian civilization since the Battle of Centennial Court, it was a tolerance they didn't want to test. To their detractors, Abidanians were superstitious and entertained ridiculous claims. But worse, the Abidanians set themselves apart. At least that is how it seemed from the outside.

"Well," Moriel concluded, "suspicions against us will certainly put a damper on our volunteer efforts."

"We could rally other communities within the city. Keep ourselves in the background," Chaz suggested.

"Mom has already begun organizing volunteers and food through her women's league. They always like being the center of these kinds of efforts," said Tyre.

"May the light of Castle Mount shine on Josephine Pruitt," said Moriel. "Get Josiah Constance involved, too. Maybe he can spare some supplies and wagons. Is the doctor available to help out?"

"They are all on top of it, sir. A caravan left just before I did."

"Thank you for letting us know about this," said Moriel. "It's a long ride from Mortinburg. Will you join your mother in Smithtown?"

"I'm not sure I will see Mom, but I do plan to help out in Smithtown after stopping in Mortinburg briefly. And you?"

"We will be there as soon as we can," Moriel assured Tyre.

Haden jumped in, "Okay, okay! Now that we've come to the aid of everyone else in Mortania, what are we going to do about Wally?"

"What's wrong with Wally?" Tyre asked.

"He's a week overdue from the Sanctuary at Miqodesh, that's

all!" Haden spewed, glaring at Moriel.

"Miqo-wah?" said Tyre.

"Miqodesh—the dwelling of the ancient ones who guard the Stone of Sages. You've been in the community for a while now, Tyre. You've never heard of the Sanctuary?" Moriel scolded lightheartedly.

"I'm sorry, Sir Moriel, I've never been a particularly good student."

"All you need to know, Tyre, is that the Sanctuary is deep in Cloakwood."

Tyre furled his brow. "Cloakwood? Few who get lost in there ever find their way out."

"Exactly!" said Haden, satisfied that at least someone could see the gravity of the situation.

Sunrays burst from the horizon and wove like a tapestry through the evergreens. Cully had already been at work for some time. He wrapped one last band of sinewy bark around the joints of a wooden stretcher and tested its strength. With a few blankets for comfort, it would do. Ander made himself useful by preparing a breakfast that could last the company hours on the trail, while Penelope and Waljan attended to Master Chen and tried to make sense of his story.

"But, sir, you said they left you alive to warn our people. Who? And what are they warning us about?" Wally asked.

"I don't know. It was like a dream. All I have is impressions. Darkness. Fire. Screams of agony and deep silence. And death."

Exasperated, Waljan took Peep aside. "I can't make any sense of this. Why can't he remember what happened less than forty-eight hours ago?"

Peep shrugged. "Maybe the whole thing was too much for him. All that's left is a bit of memory confused with snippets of nightmare—even perhaps some hallucination. It's not unexpected, considering. He's overwhelmed with grief."

"But, Peep, he's an *Agasti*. Agasti don't get overwhelmed.

31

They don't get scared. They have a steel will—they are the epitome of self-control and courage."

"I am sure he is very wise and disciplined, but he is also a frail old man," Peep said.

"Never mind. You don't understand."

"Don't I? Maybe I am just too thick-headed."

"Peep, that's not what I meant."

"I know what you meant. I am not Abidanian—not quite up to your standards. It's not the first time you've hinted at it." She stood. "I have things to do."

Penelope stomped off to find Cully. He was pulling Ander around on the stretcher. "Wow, Cull! That works great!" She hoped her enthusiasm would chase away her irritation with Wally.

"We'll have to lift it where the terrain gets rough, but with the four of us, it shouldn't be too much trouble," Cully said. "Where's Wally and Master Chen?"

"They're resting—Master Chen in his bed and Wally in his superiority."

"Wow. You two are stepping all over each other these days."

Culbert had watched Waljan and Penelope's friendship grow, flourish, and change throughout their entire lives. They were as close as any two individuals could be. But a tension had always existed between them. At times it was competitive, at other times intensely interdependent. It took the form of verbal sparring and one-upmanship. But it was hard for Penelope to dismiss her most recent conversations with Waljan as nothing more than this.

Flipping the cot upside down, Culbert playfully dumped Ander to the ground and set him to the task of filling canteens. "So what happened this time?" he asked Penelope.

Penelope picked at the needles of a nearby pine, mindlessly tossing them to the ground. "Do you ever get the feeling that Wally looks down on you because you aren't Abidanian?"

"Of course not. Do you?"

"Yeah. I do."

"Are you sure you're not just blaming him for your own feelings of not measuring up? Or maybe harboring a bit of jealousy?"

"Why should I be jealous? I can still out-hunt, out-shoot, and out-run him on a bad day."

"Yeah. But he's still the Hero of Mortinburg."

Penelope propped herself against the tree, arms crossed.

"Look," Cully continued, "there is only one thing to consider here. Do you believe in the king, or don't you? If you do, there is nothing preventing you from joining the community. If you don't, that doesn't make you less of a person. Do you think Wally would let you hang around him this long if it did?"

Penelope kicked at the ground.

Cully continued, "He has been on edge, I admit. He laid into me pretty hard yesterday. It's like he really can't accept what's happened here. But that has nothing to do with us, Peep."

Cully's words of assurance offered a bit of comfort, but Penelope still felt that he didn't quite understand. Still, she had to put her concerns aside and focus. In the wake of what would be called the Miqodesh Massacre, the group's primary task was getting Chen to safety. After much pleading and explanation, they succeeded in getting the reluctant Master Chenaniah secured in the stretcher.

The companions heaved packs onto their backs and began to drag the old master out of the village. Chen moaned deeply, "The Sanctuary has been occupied and protected for generations. I have failed the community. We have never forfeited our guardianship."

Waljan consoled him, "And you haven't still. We have the Stone with us. Every last shard has been recovered. Please try to rest."

Cully shouldered the right side of the stretcher while Waljan shouldered the left. Ander walked ahead, looking for the route that would provide the smoothest ride for Master Chen and the least trouble for Cully and Waljan. Still, it was slow going. The feet of the stretcher kept snagging on roots, stones, and brambles. From time to time, Waljan or Cully would stumble, pitching poor Chen to one side or the other. Penelope compensated by holding the side of the cot steady, but she had little leverage to counter a misstep. They went on as best they could for some time. As they passed a large Bollia tree, surrounded by fallen pods, Ander got an idea.

"Stop a minute!" he said enthusiastically.

The men set Master Chen down, happy to stretch their arms and loosen their necks and shoulders. Ander retrieved one of the remarkably large Bollia seeds from inside its pod. It was at least eight inches in diameter. Twisting a knife deeply into each end, he bored a two-inch-wide hole through the center.

"Of course! A wheel! Ander, you're brilliant," Cully said.

"We just need a shaft strong enough to support the weight of the stretcher without snapping and some cooking lard for lubricant," Ander said.

"I think we might have put your brothers in significant danger by bringing you with us, Ander," Cully suggested in jest. "I can't imagine how they're faring without you."

"Well, they won't have to for long," Ander said. "As soon as we get Master Chen to Dead Springs, I will be on my way."

"Our loss, for sure," said Cully.

Ander smiled, and everyone busied themselves with finding a suitable axle for the Bollia pod. Master Chen suggested which species of tree would likely yield the needed branch. Within a half hour, the branch was found, the wheel greased and mounted, and the spirits of all lifted. After some food and water, the band was back on the trail, making twice as much time with Ander's ingenious solution.

As the day passed, Penelope noticed that Master Chen had begun to mutter to himself. Beads of water formed on his forehead, and his eyes glazed over. Despite their efforts, Master Chen was fading.

"Wally! Cully! Can we go any faster? The master is really struggling."

Cully replied, "We are going as fast as we can, Penelope."

Penelope tried to rouse the old man. "Master Chenaniah, can you tell us a traveling story?"

He glanced over at her vaguely and said something no one could understand.

"I have an idea," Ander said, digging in his apron. "I found this poem. It fell out of one of the books back at the village. Maybe I can read it to him as we go?"

"Give it a shot," Penelope said as she dabbed the old man's forehead with a cool cloth.

Ander read:

In the now, I touch forever
What has been will ever be
Separated, still together
I in you, and you in me.

"I know this," Wally interrupted. "This is the 'Kinsmen's Ballad.' We sing it on days when we honor those who have gone before us." He continued in song:

Reaching back we can touch our future
Moving on, we can find our past.
In the Realm, there is nothing surer
Than the home we will find at last.

Master Chen's weakened garbling joined Waljan in the chorus. Soon, the entire company picked it up and they all sang together:

In the king we are one.
In the king we are one.
In the king we are family.
In the king we are one.
Each a link in the chain of freedom,
Infinite present, we reside
O'er the vastness of all being
Ever praising at his side!
In the king we are home.

In the king we are home.
In the king we have found ourselves.
In the king we are home.

The rhythm of the music found its way into the company's gait. Their voices mingled with the crunch of dried leaves and the thud of heavy feet against the damp forest floor. It lent a spark of life to Master Chen's waning breath. Before long, the travelers cleared the canopy and emerged from the eastern perimeter of Cloakwood.

"It's a clear shot from here, gang. Stay with us, Master Chen!" Wally shouted in triumph against the low groans of a rising windstorm. "Dead Springs is straight ahead. And it looks like we'll arrive just in time!"

4
Fire and Wind

A violent gust buffeted Josiah's fully loaded rig, forcing a squeak out of Josephine Pruitt. She balanced precariously like a hard-boiled egg, bouncing and rolling with the lurch of the wagon. Her impressive grip on the back of poor Josiah's overshirt kept her from being tossed out. Josiah might not have been sorry to see that, fighting as he was with the wind, the spooked horses, and Josephine's grip.

"Oh, this nasty wind! It's wreaking havoc with my hair!" the widow cried.

"Your hair is the least of our worries, madam," Josiah replied. "And I am quite sure the people of Smithtown will be too distracted with their own recovery to worry about your coiffure."

"Oh, nonsense!" Josephine argued. "A well-dressed volunteer evokes a sense of order to the chaos—an assurance that all is not lost in times of trouble."

"Are you telling me that you regard your appearance as an act of mercy?"

"That is exactly what I am telling you, Mr. Constance. And I, of all people, should know."

A number of witty but unflattering responses to Mrs. Pruitt's philosophy came to Josiah's mind but quickly dissipated with her last comment. Not only did he know too well what she had suffered in her life, he was deeply indebted to her. Josephine Pruitt was the only reason Josiah was not completely destitute after the Great Jubilee Fire that had destroyed his past, present, and future, as much as it did hers. Mrs. Pruitt financed the rebuilding and stocking of what was now Caddock General Goods in memory of her son.

The widow's generosity shocked the town. Everyone knew that Mrs. Pruitt mingled with the rich and powerful of Mortinburg, but no one had thought of her as wealthy herself. She had been considered an opportunist, one who associated with those whose good fortune she hoped would rub off on her. She was also known as romantically desperate, having never gotten over her husband's death. Whether or not it was an accurate characterization, poor Josephine was pegged as the town gold digger, a woman on the hunt for a wealthy man to marry. At least, that was her reputation until she started spending money that no one knew she had. Almost overnight she became the town philanthropist, sought after for advice, leadership and, of course, money. Several men even proposed marriage, but to everyone's surprise were turned away.

As Josiah's wagon pulled into Smithtown, followed by a caravan of volunteers and supplies from Mortinburg, Mrs. Pruitt gasped. Nearly half the town's buildings had been heavily damaged by fire and were still smoldering. Some of the building frames remained standing like blackened skeletons, gutted and threatening collapse. Others were deceptively untouched, mere facades hiding the ashen ruins that lay beyond. Several buildings were nothing more than a charred lot and a foundation.

Randomness characterized the pattern of destruction. The sooty footprints of two homes flanked the town library, which remained untouched. A business here, a bell tower there, a house around the corner—all torched. Other structures dotted throughout the town were simply passed by. Like a tornado of flame, whatever had come through the town had serpentined its way from one end to the other.

On a grassy expanse in the center of town, a large white tent fluttered in the cleansing winds that carried the smoke away to the west. The gusts dampened the normal sounds of day, lending a haunting hush to an already grim scene. As the rigs came to a halt, a young woman rushed to greet them, followed by three teenagers. She pulled at her fingers and kept her face turned from the wind. A man of about sixty years, carrying a large leather bag, hopped off one of the wagons and approached the woman to introduce himself.

"I'm Dr. Asa Fales, miss. Is that the hospital tent?"

"Yes, that is. Dr. Mallow will be so happy to see you. My brothers here can help unload the caravan."

"For love of the king, what happened here?" Dr. Fales asked.

"That's the question we are all struggling to answer, sir," the woman replied with flushing cheeks and watery eyes.

Dr. Fales addressed the brothers. "Well, gentlemen, the man in the first rig is Josiah Constance. Next to him is Josephine Pruitt. They would welcome your assistance." Then he followed the woman into the hospital tent.

Mrs. Pruitt swooned at the sight of the town. "Mr. Constance, I don't know what I was expecting, but not this. Not this. I'm feeling like I might faint."

"Now, Josephine, don't do that. The doctors have enough on their plate. Let's get you down from here." Mr. Constance climbed down and offered Mrs. Pruitt his hand.

With whimpers and flailing arms, Mrs. Pruitt stumbled over her skirts and, missing Josiah's outstretched hand entirely, practically fell into his arms with a screech. Once safely on the ground, Josephine pushed Josiah away as if it were his idea that he get assaulted by the full weight of her sizable frame. He didn't complain but recovered her handbag, which had been thrown in the tussle.

"Of all the clumsy . . . !" Mrs. Pruitt huffed, snatching the handbag away.

"Let's get to work, madam," Mr. Constance replied soberly.

Dr. Fales dug through the heavy tapestries that weighed down the hospital tent's entryway against the relentless wind. Inside, rows of men, women, and children sprawled out on mats and blankets. Amid the coughs, moans, and crying, family members spoke softly. A disheveled man circulated among the injured. He looked up at Dr. Fales.

"Please, family and medical assistance only!" he urged.

"I'm Dr. Fales. Just came in from Mortinburg."

"Oh! You are a pleasant sight, indeed. I'm Dr. Len Mallow."

The men shook hands. "Wish we were meeting in better circumstances, Dr. Mallow. Any word about the mayor?"

"No. Mayor Davenport and the sheriff are still missing. Mrs. Davenport has kept up a heroic attitude, but I'm sure she's distraught. I gave her some teas for her nerves. As you would expect, most here are suffering from smoke sickness, but we have a few severe burn cases. Some won't make it, I'm afraid. Those nearing their end have been placed in the back with their families. We are trying to make them as comfortable as we can.

"Well, what do you need from me?" asked Dr. Fales.

"Everyone who needs wound care has received it, but if you have any herbs with you that can help with pain, or supplies for mixing poultices, that would be very helpful when we need to replace dressings. If you have any ideas for how to deal with the smoke sickness, that would be great."

"I have just the supplies you need." said Dr. Fales.

A disturbance behind the tapestries drew the doctors' attention. Josiah Constance was heard scolding Mrs. Pruitt away from the tent and directing her to join the women in making food for the victims' families. She was heard huffing and stomping away, and then all fell quiet again. Mr. Constance pushed his way through the heavy rugs and stopped cold at the sight.

"What a horror," he said softly, approaching the doctors and taking in all the misery around him. "Mrs. Pruitt thinks she can be a help in here, but after losing her own son to fire, I think that would be a very bad idea."

"Agreed," said Dr. Fales. "That woman's presence might be more trouble than good here, for all of us."

"Well, let's not forget that she is the main reason the rest of us are here to help, doctor. It is an awkward thing that we are indebted to her on the one hand and disapproving of her on the other."

"True, but that fact is of her own making," said Dr. Fales.

"Well, I am certainly grateful for her contribution, gentle-men," Dr. Mallow interjected.

"In any case, we'll just have to work with the situation as it is," Dr. Fales said. "Listen, Josiah, there is a large box of herbs, concoctions, and a mortar and pestle in my rig. The box has my imprint on the side. Could you bring it in here, please?"

"Absolutely," Mr. Constance replied, and left the doctors to their work.

Down the main street, Mrs. Davenport dutifully gathered women to prepare simple meals for the victims and their fami-lies. On her way to join them, Mrs. Pruitt passed one smoldering ruin after another, slowing as she went by. Finally, she stopped in front of one building in particular. Memories of the most tragic night of her life flooded her mind. She approached the charred frame of what must have been a home.

The ghastly aroma of things not meant to feed a fire— painted wood, the shellacked faces of clay dolls, leather shoes, and horsehair brushes—filled Mrs. Pruitt's nostrils. She covered her nose with a handkerchief. Under her feet, glass from the exploded windows crunched. A quiet hiss issued from cracks in the charcoal beams, warning her that spots within were still quite hot.

Why! Why, my dear Caddock? thought Mrs. Pruitt. She recalled the excitement of that fateful night, the fun her twin sons, Tyre and Caddock, had planned and the festive atmosphere the entire town enjoyed. It was Mortinburg's Centennial Jubilee. Her memory of its tragic end—Waljan shaming Caddock into the burning Mercantile—aroused a fresh ire within her. Caddock was sent into the fire to save Josiah Constance, but Waljan reaped all the reward. Ultimately, he escaped with his life and a heroic reputation. The injustice of it fed a silent wrath befitting a protective mother.

Suddenly coming to her senses, Josephine Pruitt wiped the tears away and scolded herself, "What are you doing in here, Josephine, other than conjuring up painful ghosts?" She turned on her heels and rushed out, wiping her cheeks vigorously.

Just beyond the threshold, the shaken Mrs. Pruitt noticed the glint of a sparkling red figurine in the grass nearby. She scanned the area for prying eyes. Then, she snatched the bobble up, tucked it into her handbag, and continued on to the mayor's home.

Master Chen slept fitfully, taking shallow breaths and murmuring, "No, no! Dark . . . I can't see. No! You cannot have it! It is forbidden!" Penelope tried to ease his nightmares with soothing whispers.

The sun had just slipped below the western rim of the Crescent Mountains, and bands of orange and raspberry sky cast their warm glow through the windows of the Dead Springs Tavern and Inn. Penelope adjusted Chen's blankets and felt his forehead. Why she had so naturally stepped into the role of nursemaid, no one questioned, not even Penelope herself. But it would have been a reasonable curiosity. Penelope had never had the opportunity to serve another in this way, nor had she ever thought of doing so. There was something so magnetic in Master Chen's presence, she was simply drawn to him. She didn't know anything about him. But still, the thought that he might leave them all before she had a chance to sit and learn at his feet gave her an intense feeling of loss and waste.

The old man finally settled into a deep sleep. Penelope quietly stepped out of the room and joined the men in the tavern, where a battle of wills raged.

"We can't let the boy go on by himself, Moriel!" Haden

insisted.

"Are you afraid I won't return the horse, sir?" Ander said. "My brothers are rough, but they are not thieves. They are honest men. And so am I."

"Look, kid. This is not about the horse. You're nothing but a scrap of a lad, and in a half hour it will be darker than pitch outside," Haden said. "And then this windstorm!" He ended his rant in a fit of coughing that forced him into a chair.

"But my brothers are out there *in this windstorm*," Ander stated emphatically. "I have to go back, with or without your help. I didn't ask to come here. And Wally promised I would return. It's been too long already. Even if they aren't in danger, what will they think if I don't return?"

"Ander is right, Haden. You both are," said Moriel. "Cully, Chaz, are you willing to accompany the boy back to his brothers?"

The men agreed.

"Okay, then," Moriel said. "Cully and Ander can take the horses from Haden's rig. We need to stay here anyway while we figure out what we do next and help Master Chen regain his strength."

"Do you think he will, Sir Moriel?" Peep asked.

"Of course he will!" Wally interrupted. "Sir Moriel is known as one of the finest healers in Mortania. He brought me back to life, anyway."

"You are being a little dramatic, aren't you, Wally?" Moriel laughed.

"Well if I am, it's fitting. I nearly drowned! It took me weeks to get back on my feet. But I did, thanks to Sir Moriel."

"Well, being young and healthy worked to your advantage. Master Chenaniah is a different case altogether. But he has a strong will and a purpose. If the king wishes for his continued service in Mortania, we will do our best to keep him here."

After a much-deserved, and much-needed meal, everyone sprang into motion. Insisting that Cully bring Bo Dog with him, Waljan fed the faithful lab and said his goodbyes. Moriel prepared a healing infusion for Master Chen, and Cully and Chaz saddled and loaded the horses.

Ander pulled Penelope aside. "I have something for you."

"For me?" she said in surprise.

"Well, sort of. I think you will be interested in it. But we should probably return it to Master Chen. It belongs to the Sanctuary. Could you give it to him?"

"Certainly I will," said Peep.

"But I think you should read it, first. You and I—well, we are kind of in the same situation."

"What do you mean, Ander?"

"We're servant-hearts."

Penelope bristled at the idea, squinting and scrunching up her nose.

"We are!" Ander emphasized. "I follow my brothers around. I take orders. I do things that no one else will do because no one else will do them. In fact, they don't even realize these things need doing. Without me, life would be much more difficult for them. But they don't realize that. And that's okay. We servant-hearts know we're the glue that holds the works together. And though we are merely overlooked servants in the opinions of most people, we are just important in a different way, you know?"

"I'm no one's servant, Ander," Peep insisted.

"You are. I think that's why I like you so much more than the others. You follow Wally. You tend to Master Chen. You help when it's needed even when it's not asked for or noticed—just like you did at Miqodesh. The servant-hearts are heroes, too."

Penelope felt heat rise in her cheeks but giggled dismissively. "You're kinda weird, Ander, you know?"

Ander smiled, handing Penelope a book. "Anyway, I picked this out of a pile tossed from one of the Sanctuary huts. I have been reading it since we got here. I would take it with me, but it isn't mine to keep."

"I will make sure Chen gets it, Ander."

Cully called from the horses. "Ander, let's go, my young friend!" Ander trotted over to his horse. Cully helped him up.

"Ride safe," Peep said. "Listen for cracking branches in this wind!"

As the three rode off into the inky night, Penelope looked down at the book. The edges were singed, and the linen cover dusty with charcoal ash; but she could clearly read the title: *Nava—A Servant's Heart*.

Returning to the master's bedside, Penelope felt his steady pulse. The room had grown cold. Penelope started a fire in the hearth and sat down in a worn, upholstered chair by the window. A tree branch tapped rhythmically against the window and then quieted with each gust of wind that whisked it farther away.

With her feet dangling over the arms of the chair, Penelope cracked the book open and started to read about the life of Nava of the Realm, a young girl who served the king by doing nothing of great note. The idea confused Penelope, and she tossed the book aside. Wally had taught her to read, but it wasn't something she found practically useful. It certainly wasn't worth the effort to read a book that made no sense.

But the irony of being celebrated in writing for no particular reason needled Penelope's brain to the point that she had to make sense of it. She picked up the book, grabbed a blanket from the foot of Master Chen's bed, and nestled back in the chair. She was determined to finish one chapter, at least.

The wind howled. The fire crackled. Within the hour the weariness of a long and busy day won out. Penelope was fast asleep.

5
Scene of the Crime

Tyre Pruitt expected a hive of activity at Smithtown but rode instead into ghostly stillness. He noticed the rigs, parked in a row, that had brought in much-needed aid from Mortinburg. After dismounting, Tyre led his foaming horse into an untended corral, stocked with water, grain, and hay. He unfastened the saddle, pulled it off the horse, and heaved it over a fence rung. Then, he set off to help with the relief effort.

By now, all the smoldering destruction had turned ashen and cold. Many buildings had toppled as the embers ate through whatever support remained. It would be many weeks before the damage was removed and new building begun.

The most conspicuous structure in town was the temporary hospital tent, which stood out like a big white elephant. Guessing its purpose, Tyre peeked his head in quietly. Many of the cots lay empty, while others were occupied by recovering victims. A couple of attendants acknowledged him with a nod. Tyre gave them a quick wave and continued deeper into town.

He passed the charred frame of a home and stopped. Out in the yard, a little girl with big, bouncing curls and dressed in formal black with dainty leather slippers walked slowly through the grass, singing, "Daniella, where are you? Where did you go? Daniella, where are you, where did you go?"

"Hello," Tyre said kindly.

"Hello, sir," the girl curtseyed. She continued her song.

"What are you doing?" Tyre asked.

"I am looking for Daniella."

"Is Daniella your . . . little sister?"

The little girl stopped just long enough to say, "I don't have a little sister."

"Oh. Well. Who is Daniella, then?"

"My dragon."

"Well, if you are looking for a dragon, shouldn't you be searching the sky rather than the grass?"

"My dragon doesn't fly," the little girl said, her eyebrows and nose scrunched together. "Daniella's wings are too stiff!"

"Of course," Tyre replied, trying to appear as serious as possible. "Silly of me."

"I think I dropped her in the grass." The little girl returned to her search and her song.

Tyre looked around for any sign of the girl's parents or a guardian. "Where is your family?"

The little girl stopped singing and straightened. She looked toward the west end of town. Staring a moment, she turned and bolted in the opposite direction.

"Wait!" Tyre yelled after her. But the little girl disappeared around a corner. Tyre walked west in hopes of finding someone he knew. Winding to the left, the main street sloped down to an expansive yard where a large group of people stood among an army of gravestones. The crowd encircled a woman who spoke loudly and deliberately. A row of freshly dug graves spread out beside her.

Searching the crowd from the road above, Tyre spotted his mother standing apart. She seemed unsure whether to share in the mourning or protect her own heart from it. The image took Tyre's thoughts back to his brother's funeral. But this was not the time to relive his own pain. He choked down the tears, took a deep breath, and walked down to join Josephine Pruitt.

Tyre greeted her solemnly. "Mother." Mrs. Pruitt blinked her ambivalence in return. "Even now you are going to shun me?"

"Shunning is what *your* people do, dear. Now, please, let's show some respect for the deceased and remain quiet."

Taking her reproach for the sake of decorum, Tyre thought it best to seek others he may know from the crowd to avoid the inevitable argument that his mother would indulge. Tyre loved his mother deeply. He shared so much of her grief and understood the measure that he did not share. But that did not protect him from her estrangement.

Although their father died months before Tyre and his brother were born, Bartholomew Pruitt was a part of Tyre's daily life through his mother's suffering. Suffering had become Mrs. Pruitt's third child. She coddled it, nourished it, and allowed it to grow into a healthy resentment.

A hushed bustle grew among the crowd. "Where is Hazel? . . . Hazel!" Tyre moved toward the voice to find an old woman frantically searching among the people.

"Excuse me, ma'am, but what does Hazel look like?" he asked.

"She is a little girl of five years. Light, curly hair and a little black dress," whispered the woman.

"I think I spoke to her. She was playing in the front lawn of one of the burned-out homes, looking for a dragon named Daniella."

"Yes, that would be her! Thank you, young man. That child will be the death of me! And then what is she going to do, I ask you?" The woman bustled off.

The service concluded, and the funeral director introduced Mrs. Pruitt to the crowd. She pushed her way through, and after patting some stray hairs around her tightly twisted bun, announced the availability of refreshments back at the mayor's mansion. As the crowd slowly broke up and headed toward the mayor's home, raindrops joined a chorus of inconsolable weeping.

Tyre stood, studying the faces of those who passed him. He recognized Josiah Constance, who stuck his hand out.

"Tyre Pruitt, you made it safely to Dead Springs, I presume?"

"Yes, sir. Haden and Moriel will be there awhile. Haden fears they've lost Wally."

"Lost Wally?"

"In the woods. Apparently, Wally is on some kind of errand. They're afraid he lost his way in Cloakwood."

"That's unlikely," Mr. Constance said.

"You know Haden, sir. Especially these days. He's very easily agitated. I'm sure he's just exaggerating."

"How concerned did Sir Moriel appear?"

"Not at all," Tyre said with confidence.

"There you go. I'm sure Waljan Woodland is just fine. Are you here to stay awhile and help?"

"Yes sir. Wherever I can."

"Fine. I think Dr. Fales could use it. Thank you for finding little Hazel. I saw you chatting with her grandmother. That poor woman has been through so much. Hazel is all she has left. The entire family was lost in the fire."

"Mr. Constance, does anyone have any idea what happened that night?"

"None. People are saying it was as if the fires combusted spontaneously all at once, as if someone just snapped his fingers. By the time anyone realized the danger, the buildings were fully engulfed."

"How did Hazel escape? She doesn't seem to have a single injury," Tyre said.

"Well, that's a puzzle. Apparently, the little girl wasn't in the house at the time."

"But I thought the fires happened late at night?"

"Yes. Doc Mallow thinks she may have been sleepwalking," Mr. Constance said. "Now, I don't know about you, but I am nearly soaked through. Let's get over to the mayor's and warm up with a cup of tea."

The two men headed over to the mayor's home and squeezed in, winding their way over to the kitchen. It seemed that the entire town was present in this sprawling home that should have felt roomier. A group of ladies, mostly volunteers from Mortinburg, bustled around to keep the plates of appetizers and punch bowls filled. Huddles of quiet conversation gathered here and there. Little Hazel was seated in a corner, her grandmother hovering over her with a plate of carrots and little sandwiches.

As Tyre poured himself a cup of hot tea, he felt several pairs of eyes staring him down. The conversation became quieter until all of Tyre's attention was drawn to the hiss of whispers. He heard the word *Assassin*. Then, a question that started "Isn't he . . ." and faded away. Mrs. Pruitt looked up from dishing some deviled eggs, her eyes darting from one gawker to the next. Finally, someone spoke up.

"Hey. I know you. You're one of those Abidanians," said a man with a mouth full of stuffed mushrooms.

Tyre turned to the speaker and offered his hand. "Yes, sir. My name is Tyre. . . ."

"I have no interest in your name. I've heard that one of your kind is responsible for this misery. I buried my aunt and cousins today."

A woman added, "I lost my husband!"

"And my best friend!" said another.

"I am very sorry . . . ," Tyre began. But he was interrupted again.

"We don't need your sympathy. We need to know what you are doing here. Revisiting the scene of the crime?"

Josiah began to move between the man and Tyre, concerned that the emotion of the week might get the better of the people's good sense.

"Sir, I am here to help," Tyre assured the man.

"Yeah? Well, we don't want your help. You need to go."

Then another man spoke up. "No! Don't let him go. He has to answer for this. We need justice!"

Tyre frantically looked to his mother, who had obviously earned the townspeople's trust and gratitude. She looked away and left the room. Before Tyre knew what had happened, Josiah had been pushed out of the way and the room erupted in angry accusations. They seized Tyre and took him outside in a riot of violent commotion. Dr. Mallow and Dr. Fales darted out of the hospital tent to quiet the crowd that dragged Tyre along as it passed by. As if of one mind, the doctors ran to the head of the crowd.

"What are you people doing?" Dr. Mallow yelled.

The leader of the pack explained their intentions to seek justice for their loved ones. If they couldn't punish Tyre themselves, they would at least throw him in jail.

"For what?" Dr. Mallow cried.

"The boy is an Abidanian! Word is that the Shadow Assassin is Abidanian, crawling out from the bowels of Castle Mount. He comes out at night from a hole in the ground to destroy and murder. The kid has to know something!"

"You people don't know what you're talking about!" Tyre yelled.

Dr. Fales cut in, "Friends, please. I know you are all upset and want to get to the bottom of this. I know you need closure and to understand how this tragedy happened. But you don't want to take your pain out on this innocent boy."

"We can at least get the truth out of him!" said someone from the back.

And then another, "To the river! We can make him talk!"

Suddenly, a crack split the air, and everyone jumped back. "Enough!" boomed a voice from a surprisingly small, dark man with a weathered face. In his hand, he loosely bobbed the grip of a black leather whip. "Haven't we had enough? Everyone back to your homes. I want this street cleared. After all this week has brought us, after all your own family and friends still suffer, lying in the hospital tent, listening to your anger and hate, don't ya think we can afford a little peace? I'll take it from here."

"You're not the sheriff!" someone in the crowd yelled.

"No, but he's not here and I'm the next best thing. In fact, according to city ordinance 5016.329, as deputy I assume the sheriff's post until he is located. Now, move on!"

Disgruntled and emotionally spent, the crowd trickled away. Len Mallow returned to the tent, while Dr. Fales stayed by Tyre's side.

"Thank you," Dr. Fales said to the lawman.

"I'm not doing you a favor; I'm keeping order. Just gonna throw the kid in jail anyway. But at least this way he'll get there in one piece."

"Throw him in jail? He's been in town less than an hour! What are the charges?" Dr. Fales asked.

"Well, we can start with disturbing the peace and inciting a riot until I think up something better."

"I don't like the sound of that," Dr. Fales admitted.

"Don't worry, doc. We aren't going to allow any volunteers from Mortinburg to get strung up for nothing. I just want things to settle down. I'm just one man against a crowd. Know what I mean?"

Dr. Fales nodded tentatively, patting Tyre on the shoulder. "Don't worry. We'll get this straightened out."

The man took Tyre by the arm and led him toward the jailhouse. The whole thing was like a weird nightmare. Tyre stared at the lawman's rugged features, incredulous. The crooked nose had once been straight and dignified, and the leathery, pocked complexion was once smooth. Tyre knew this face. It was the face of trouble.

"You're Bruce Malvo," Tyre said.

"*Deputy* Malvo. Although, I am betting that will soon be Sheriff Malvo."

"Do you remember me?" asked Tyre too impulsively to

doubt the wisdom of that question.

"Of course I do, kid," Malvo chuckled. "Why do you think I'm locking you up?"

6

Enemies Within

Long before sunrise, Waljan followed Moriel and Haden down a creaking wooden staircase at the back of the tavern. The drafts, sweet and earthy, cooled with each step. Waljan shivered with the unexpected change in temperature, from the heated tavern to the dark, dank cellar.

At the base of the stairs, rows of wooden barrels lined the walls on shelves from floor to ceiling. Each barrel was labeled with a date and the contents: ales, wines, infusions, and herbal brews for medicinal uses. When they had come to the second to last section of shelves, Moriel and Haden pushed against it on either end. With a click, the entire section and the wall behind it gave way, sliding inward on a hidden track. It opened into a passage to the right.

Waljan's eyes widened. "Where in the world are we going? I feel like a grave robber discovering a hidden crypt."

"Grab three torches from the corner there, Wally, and remain quiet for a time," Moriel instructed in a hushed voice. Wally obeyed, and Moriel lit each torch, handing one to Haden and taking one for himself. "Now stay close," he whispered. "We have a bit of a hike, and without these torches, there is absolutely no visibility down here."

Waljan had never been in a blacker space. Within a foot or

two from the flame, the darkness swallowed up the torchlight. It was suffocating. Waljan's breath echoed off the walls, and he couldn't tell if the thumping came from his feet or his heart. Even so, he was eager to follow Sir Moriel anywhere.

Although Haden had raised Waljan, Moriel was the boy's mentor and hero. Both men were indispensable anchors in Waljan's life. Despite the claustrophobic discomfort of these tunnels, Waljan would choose to be nowhere else. His very identity was entwined with the lives of these two men.

"Do you know of anyone fainting down here, Moriel? Because if not, I may be the first!" Waljan said.

"Shhhhh . . . ," said Moriel. "We must remain quiet in the tunnels."

"Oh, great," Waljan whispered. "So we're deaf, mute, *and* blind!"

"Not completely. Just follow the torchlight, Wally. You'll be fine. Best not to speak until you smell the salt air."

"But why?" Waljan insisted.

"Your curiosity is ill timed, Waljan. But if it will silence your worries as well as your voice, I'll tell you. We are traveling a secret network of underground passageways that have protected the coastal Abidanians of Dead Springs for generations. Using this system presents a risk to them, but it's the only way to reach our destination. We do what we can to avoid exposing them."

Satisfied and a little ashamed, Waljan fell silent. The three trudged along for what seemed like miles. It was difficult to determine how long they'd been down there. Nothing changed. The air was deathly still. Though Waljan knew he was progressing forward, his eyes could not confirm that he'd traveled any distance at all. It was oddly like walking in place.

Then, he noticed that the ground under his feet began to shift. Each step required a little more effort, and the sound of his footsteps softened. The air began to stir slightly, and the oppressive darkness lifted just enough for Waljan to make out the walls on either side of him.

Haden dropped his torch and, for the third time since entering the tunnels, leaned over on his knees, gripped by spasmodic coughs.

"Everything all right there, Haden?" Moriel asked. Waljan ran to Haden's side, but the old man waved him off. "We'll give you a few minutes, Haden. Try to relax a bit," Moriel said, sitting down against the cavern wall and plunging his torch into the sandy floor. Waljan plopped down next to him.

"He's very sick, isn't he," Wally whispered to Moriel. "His cough is worsening."

"He insists it's nothing, Wally. But I'm keeping an eye on him. Stubborn old codger that he is, he wouldn't admit being sick until he was dead." Sensing Waljan stiffen up, Moriel assured him, "Don't worry, Wally. Didn't you say I was a master healer?"

Waljan smiled, and his shoulders eased up just as Haden finally recovered his breath. The old hunter shuffled over and slowly tucked in next to the other two with a deep sigh.

"Well, I'm not getting any younger, that's for sure, gentlemen!" Haden said cheerfully. They all sat quietly for a time.

Discomfort needled Waljan. He stood. "Shouldn't we keep moving, Moriel? Haden's coughing might be a problem."

"Good point, Wally." Moriel lent Haden a hand, and they continued on their way, trudging through the deepening sand.

Ambient light gained on the darkness. Waljan quickened his pace and then stopped. Breathing in deeply, he detected a new freshness and then the briny hint of sea air.

"We must be close to the coast," Wally whispered.

"Yes. All clear!" Moriel replied.

"And none too soon," Haden said as he approached. He had fallen behind and hobbled up to them, wheezing.

"I've never been to the sea," Waljan said.

"This isn't exactly a vacation spot, Wally," Moriel said. "This is a treacherous coast. The bones of ancient ships and men lie below waters so turbulent that even the barnacles fail to thrive. But it's offered additional protection to those who live here."

The three had come to a fork in the tunnel. To the right, Waljan could hear the faint whooshing of the breakers and to the left, the hollow rhythm of dripping water. The companions took the left branch, which eased down a slight incline and emerged in a sea cave much like the Abidanian caverns of Mortinburg.

The waters of a mist pool rippled in the center of the room and reflected torchlight back against the walls. The pool, different from any that Waljan had seen before, was constructed entirely of sagestone, gleaming white with pearly accents. Set atop a pedestal, this pool was smaller than usual. It contained no edges but curved gracefully from base to bowl.

Circling the pool, a pictorial history of Abidanian traditions and beliefs played out on the cave walls. It captivated Waljan. The story of Castle Wall and the birth of Mortania were skillfully carved into the rock and brightly painted. Above and below, glyphs and symbols told other tales that Waljan could not decipher.

From the darkness came a voice: "Allegiance to him who waits."

Moriel replied, "To him who waits in the mist."

"Moriel, Haden! Welcome."

"Thank you for meeting us here, old friend," Moriel replied.

A wild-looking fellow with long wisps of white hair moved into the orange light. He was weathered and wizened, but looked remarkably young in body, as if the briny air had preserved him. By his clear amber eyes, one could tell that he was full of vigor. He scrutinized Waljan for a few seconds.

"So, this is Waljan of the Realm, Hero of Mortinburg, is it?"

"Yes, sir," Waljan replied.

Haden introduced the man. "Wally, this is Sir Eban, elder of the Twelve of Dead Springs."

Waljan nodded respectfully.

"You bring a heavy sadness with you, my brothers," Eban said.

"Yes, we do," said Moriel. "The shards of the Stone of Sages."

A man of his shade could hardly get any paler, but Eban did, even so. "*Shards*?" he asked. "It is worse than I feared. Our speaking stones went silent, but I didn't suspect this. The Stone of Sages is virtually indestructible. It's protected by the power and wisdom of the Agasti of Miqodesh. This is very distressing news."

"It is. But there is more. The Agasti are dead. Or missing. Only one survives, Master Chenaniah. Whatever destroyed the Stone destroyed the Sanctuary as well. That is why we are here. We've learned nothing from the master. He is very ill and shut up like a clam."

"It's his shame. He believes he has violated his vows to protect the Stone."

"Yes. I'm afraid so."

"Who would do such a thing? And why?" Eban turned to Waljan. "You were there, son. You must be able to tell us something."

Waljan's throat tightened up. He wasn't convinced his elders would understand. Moreover, he wasn't certain that his absence was justified. Wrestling with himself, he finally reasoned that the full truth could wait.

"I was not there, sir," said Wally.

"Not there? But you were sent on our behalf to take counsel with the Agasti. You were scheduled to be there many days before this attack, if my stone is any indication." The disappointment in Sir Eban's eyes was painfully evident to Waljan.

"Yes, sir. I was ambushed by a gang of bounty hunters. It was a case of mistaken identity, but they would not listen to reason."

"I see. We must confer with our witnesses. The Sages will speak."

"The Sages, Sir Eban?" Moriel asked.

"If it is as we suspect, the Agasti have entered the Realm and have received their mantle as royal Sages. Perhaps they will tell us what happened."

Haden and Moriel exchanged glances.

"Sir Eban," Moriel said. "You understand that the Stone was completely shattered?"

"Yes, you made that quite clear to me. You have the entire stone even if in pieces, no?"

"We expect so. But mending it would be impossible. And even if we could, we don't have the gift of Seeing."

"You and I don't. But I have heard that Waljan of the Realm does. It's my understanding that our young knight has stepped right through the mist and into the Realm itself. He is the only one in my lifetime that has entered the Realm and returned. Is that true, Waljan?"

"An exaggeration, sir. I have had visions. Perhaps nothing more than my own imagination," Waljan said.

"Well, let's see what we can find. Come, bring the shards." Eban took the bag of shards from Moriel and gently eased the shattered stone into the mist pool. The larger pieces rolled erratically to the center of the bowl and settled there.

Eban closed his eyes and spoke quiet words no one could discern as the plunk of dripping water bounced off the rugged walls. "Now we will invoke the mist," he said quietly. The men sang the summoning chant, raising a cloud above the bowl. "Come, Waljan of the Realm," Eban gently commanded. "Approach the pool." Waljan complied. "Tell us what you see."

Waljan placed his hands on the edge of the bowl. Engulfed in mist, he stood motionless for several minutes. His eyes then began to flit left and right. In his mind a flurry of images raced by. A few Waljan recognized: a hooded form, a blazing firestorm, a snapping rope, a growling coyote. Disconnected and meaningless, they came and went in endless waves.

"Well, Wally, what do you see?" Haden asked.

"Peace, Haden," Eban softly reprimanded. "He can't hear you. Be patient."

Waljan continued to stare, entranced as his face scrunched up in pain. He began to tremble. Within the confused vision, a shapeless menace turned, laughing, and approached. It wore a speaking stone pouch around what might have been its neck. Agasti, bound in coils of rope, stared eerily at Waljan and wept. Then they faded as snarling jaws bit through the image and snapped at Waljan's face. He flinched, stumbling backward out of the mist and into Haden's arms. With an alarming and guttural shout, Waljan shook Haden off. He ran for the opening of the chamber. Then, slowing, he stopped. With his hands on his knees, he propped himself up, hanging his head and gulping down air.

"Waljan?" Sir Eban said.

Waljan turned around, mystified, as if he'd forgotten the others were there.

"Wally, what did they say?" Moriel pressed.

Vaguely, like one recalling a distant dream, Wally said, "Nothing. They said nothing. They just wept. Just as they did before."

"Before?" Eban inquired.

"I saw them in the longhouse at Miqodesh when we first discovered the Stone." Wally said, still trancelike.

"Did you see anything else?" Haden asked.

Waljan looked up, his eyes wide and watery. "There was darkness and fire. Terror. And . . . evil."

"What do you mean?" Eban asked. "Like a presence, a feeling?"

Recovering, Waljan straightened up. "A person," he said with certainty. "An evil person. It was the Shadow Assassin."

"You *saw* him?" Moriel asked.

"No . . . yes? I don't know what I saw. It was chaotic—confused—just as Master Chen described."

"Master Chen described nothing, Wally. That is why we're here," Moriel said.

"I know. I didn't understand then, either. But now I do and yet I can't tell you why. I'm sorry, Moriel, I can only tell you what I saw."

"But you just said you don't know what you saw!"

"Why are you jumping all over me, Moriel? I am doing the

best I can. Why don't you look into the mist and tell me what *you* see?"

Haden intervened. "Moriel, Wally has had a hard few days."

"You don't need to apologize for me, Haden. I am not imagining anything. I just can't describe it clearly, but I know what it meant."

"It meant nothing!" Moriel said forcefully. "The Stone of Sages is shattered. It's unreliable."

"It is not the Stone that speaks, Moriel," said Sir Eban.

"Well, then why place it in the mist pool?" Haden asked.

"For safety, my dear huntsman," Eban explained. "It is not commonly known that the Twelve of Dead Springs are commissioned to dispose of sagestone artifacts. Seldom is it needed. But our mist pool is specially carved to neutralize the erratic energy discharge of sagestone fragments. You are all quite lucky to have carried them so far without injuring yourselves. As for Waljan's vision, what he sees is quite reliable as long as we interpret it correctly. It is the Sages who speak through the Stone. We would be wise to listen."

"Unfortunately we must listen through the inexperienced ears of a neophyte. There is no Shadow Assassin," Moriel insisted. "Wally is just parroting Smithtown hysterics. A similar attack occurred there this week."

Wally shook his head. "I don't understand your distrust in me, Moriel. I may be a neophyte, but I am sure about this. Not only is the assassin real. He is one of us. He's Abidanian."

7

A Servant's Heart

The cool morning light snuck into the room and gently nudged Penelope. She hadn't moved since seeing the men off to Cloakwood the night before. Like an overgrown hermit crab, she unfolded herself and slowly stretched the ache out of her limbs and neck. She had slept too deeply.

"So you are alive, after all?" Master Chen sat up against a mountain of pillows.

"It seems we both are, sir!" Peep responded with a grin. "But I think sleeping in this chair was a bad idea." She grimaced as she rose and limped over to the old sage, her right leg buzzing and her foot completely numb. "Can I get you something to eat?"

"Oh, no, no, thank you. I ate hours ago. It seems you have . . . how do they say it around here . . . oh yes, you have 'held the moon for ransom.'"

"What time is it?" Peep asked, wide-eyed.

"Midday at least."

"Well, someone has been taking good care of you while I dreamed the morning away."

The old man nodded. "The good knight Moriel has been practicing his healing skills, and I am feeling much relieved and comforted, thank you. What is it you guard so dearly?" Master Chen asked, pointing to the book Penelope still clutched in her hands, unaware.

"Oh! This is for you," Penelope said. "Ander salvaged it from the Sanctuary. He wanted you to have something to remember." She handed the book to Master Chen.

"That is very kind of the boy, Penelope. But I am not certain that is a night I want to remember. Still . . ." Master Chen paused to leaf through the fragile, singed pages. "Perhaps our young friend has a bit of the Realm in him? He has chosen a most excellent sage to read. Nava. She reminds me of you."

"That's what Ander said," Penelope replied. "But, she's nothing like me—she's just a housemaid. Nothing very heroic about that."

Master Chen raised his eyebrows and chuckled. "No? There are as many ways to be heroic as there are ways to be. She may not wield a sword, but I suspect Nava has much to tell you."

"Me? I don't see how a book can tell me anything useful that I haven't learned by experience."

"I didn't suggest the *book* had anything to say," Chen clarified.

"Well, of course, but . . ." Penelope shook her head and scrunched up her pixie nose as she did every time she puzzled over an idea.

"You don't understand how the dead can teach the living?"

"That, yes. But . . . even if she could, why would this Nava want to talk to me? I'm not even Abidanian."

"Miss Penelope, look around you. Are not your closest friends Abidanian? Aren't I?"

"I didn't mean any disrespect, sir."

"I realize that. You misunderstand me. What separates you from an Abidanian is nothing more than a decision. Everyone belongs to the Realm, whether or not they realize or acknowledge it." Penelope's brow furrowed. Master Chen continued, "You have a family?"

"Just Cully," Peep said.

"Well, if you and your brother had been raised apart, would

you still be members of the same family?"

"I guess so, yeah."

"And would you not want to be reunited with your brother, had you learned of his existence?"

"Probably," Peep replied.

"It is the same with the king," said Master Chen. "He has been separated from his people, and many do not know him. But we are still his subjects. He ceded the land we occupy to Uriel, but he did not cede his people. You see, a sovereign king serves willing subjects. But a tyrant rules by force. What makes us his people has more to do with his love for us than our knowledge of him. We are his people—his *family*—for that is what he wants us to be."

"Wally has told me a little about the history of Mortania and the great walls that surround Castle Mount. But he never told me that it was *my* history or that I belonged within those walls. Honestly, I never thought I was worthy to enter the Realm."

Master Chenaniah smiled. "That is what Uriel wants you to think. But even the most insignificant of us are treasures in the eyes of the king."

"You Abidanians always talk about this Uriel. The towns of Mortania are independent states, each with their own governments. If the king gave Mortania to Uriel, where is he and why doesn't anyone else seem to know about him?"

"It's a good question, Penelope. One cannot underestimate the historical influence of the king. The people long to serve their sovereign in love, not in fear. A tyrant can only rule by fear. So Uriel hides, quietly and subtly sowing fear and hatred among the people in the hopes that one day, when mankind is stripped of courage and love, he can reign uncontested.

"First, he convinces them that they have the power to rule themselves—to reject the leadership of their sovereign. That opens the door to competition, corruption, division, and war. Then, he proposes to bring order to that chaos through power and oppression. At times he has succeeded. And other times he's been defeated. But he never gives up. And that is the great struggle of our lives."

Penelope sat quietly, allowing the explanation to play out in her imagination. Chen rested his head back on his pillow and said, "All this discussion has drained me. I should rest." He handed the book back to Penelope. "Finish the book. Then you will know whether or not Nava has anything useful to say."

The rhythm of galloping horses drew Penelope to the window. A large flock of crows dispersed from trees lining the road, and a band of horseman approached the inn. At the head was Ander and a large ogre of a man. Just behind them Penelope could make out Cully and Chaz, followed by a motley entourage.

"Cully! Ander!" Peep yelled out the window, waving. "I'll be back, sir."

"Take your time, young lady. I'm not going anywhere."

Penelope skipped downstairs. Waljan, Haden, and Moriel had recently returned from the caverns, and by the time Penelope reached the porch, they were already outside greeting the party.

"What's all this?" Moriel asked.

Ander jumped from his mount and bounced over to Moriel with a big smile. "Sir Moriel of the Realm, I would like you to meet my brothers. This is Mack Slade, and back there is Ike."

"An' I'm Fenek!" boomed a voice from the back of the company, followed by a bit of commotion as the bumbling brute pushed his way through, headed straight for Waljan, and clapped him hard on the back. "Remember me, kid?"

Mack dismounted and approached. Sizing up Moriel, he nodded a tense greeting. The hair on the back of Wally's neck rose, but he was sure there was no real threat. Mack exceeded Moriel in height and weight, but Wally would bet on Moriel having the upper hand in combat.

Mack took note of Moriel's long brown robe and fine weapon. "So, you are Moriel, the legendary Knight of Abidan. I have heard many stories," Mack said with sardonic admiration. "I didn't imagine you in a dress."

"And I didn't imagine you having the ability to form words," Moriel retorted. "We are both pleasantly surprised." Waljan broke out in a muffled laugh he tried to control.

Mack smiled, slightly amused by Moriel's willingness to push back. "It's seems that we owe you."

"A debt or payback?" Haden asked, leaning up against the porch rail with his fingers tucked casually in his front pockets.

"Your Waljan is a man of his word," Mack replied.

"That he is," Moriel said. "But why have you come here? You could have been on your way. You're not trying to reclaim him, are you?"

"Nah. Seems we had the wrong man," Mack admitted. "We were hoping you'd be interested in helping us track down the right one." Not getting the reaction he expected, Mack thought it necessary to clarify. "Maweth. The Shadow Assassin."

Moriel started to laugh.

"It wouldn't be easy, but you would be performing a good deed," said Mack.

"Really?" Moriel challenged. "You mean for the good of Mortania, or the good of your wallets?"

"Aren't they the same thing, after all?"

Waljan couldn't help but voice the deep disdain he had for the Slade brothers after his experiences in Cloakwood. "I don't know that we want to help men like you."

Mack crossed his arms and squinted one eye. "And what kind of men are we?"

"The kind that will get a little too rowdy in the middle of the night and beat up on boys half their size. Boys they are responsible for protecting."

"You don't see him complaining, do you?" Mack said, glancing back at the boy. Ander stared back at his brother with a pleading expression until Mack explained. "Look. Ander and I had a good heart-to-heart on our way back here. And the boys and I are cleaning up our act."

"That true, Ander?" Moriel asked. Ander nodded, walking

over to Mack's side. Moriel continued, "I am glad to know that. Even so, we don't hunt down rumors. I'm sure you've run into some pretty shadowy characters in your day. Maweth is not among them."

With unsettling gravity Mack argued, "Now there you're wrong."

Moriel turned and started for the tavern door when Chaz stopped him. "Sir Moriel, is there not a Council of Twelve here in Dead Springs?"

"There is," Moriel said, turning back around.

"I think it would be wise to meet with them. Give Mack a chance to share his experience with a number of us. Whether or not the Shadow Assassin is real, there is something out there. We need to figure out what it is and what it's up to. Don't you think?"

Moriel considered Chaz's words. Looking over at Haden, then Wally and Penelope, he could tell that general agreement hung in the air. "Okay. I'll arrange a council with Sir Eban. But we were supposed to be back in Mortinburg over a week ago. We need to let the community know that our mission has changed."

"I'll go," Chaz offered.

The Abidanians of Dead Springs were fewer than those of Mortinburg. But their history was ancient and rich. It was written that after the Great Separation, a small band loyal to the king fled to the sea. They hid among the sea caves east of what is now Dead Springs, surviving on shellfish and underground fresh water pools.

According to legend, an entire civilization grew out of an intricate network of connected cave dwellings. The members came topside only in the evening to forage. Rumors circulated that these were the dead leaving their graves at night in search of human prey. And that was all that remained of this great civilization: ghost stories and folklore. At least, that is what most believed.

Yet, twelve of these mysterious cave dwellers greeted Moriel, his men, and the Slade brothers in a hidden lodge among the northeastern hills above Dead Springs. The elders sat around the curved edge of a crescent table with Sir Eban at the center. Each looked ancient and wise, grizzled by the salty air. There was no mistaking their unity. With folded hands resting serenely in front of them and eyes fixed solidly on whomever had the floor at the time, each man seemed like a slight variation on a theme, or a different edition of the same book.

Mack addressed them: "The Shadow Assassin, Maweth, has been on the move for some time."

Moriel was quick to interrupt. "Maweth died many years ago, and much of what we know of him is legend and superstition."

"That's what you say. Others say different. No one ever saw the body. Stories about his violent end differ from region to region, and many claim he's been lying low," Mack said.

Waljan tried to interject but Moriel waved him off, saying, "Like I said, Mr. Slade, legend, superstition, and fantasy."

"Make-believe villains don't start real fires," said Mack.

One of the twelve elders agreed with Moriel. "The Shadow is unfortunately the invention of overzealous and superstitious Abidanians. Sometimes a fire is just a fire. Our job as subjects of the king is to serve the people of Mortania, not to validate rumors."

"Yeah, well, I'm not an Abidanian, I'm a bounty hunter," Mack countered. "And rumors don't pay the bills. I chase plenty of flesh-and-blood bad guys every day. It's what I do. And I am telling you all that Maweth is a flesh-and-blood bad guy."

"If I may, gentlemen," another elder interjected. "It seems to me that any conclusions about the cause of these fires is premature. And using those conclusions to criticize our own Abidanian brothers and sisters not only distracts from our aim here but causes discord among the king's people. If I remember correctly, this kind of criticism and discord is why Sir Waljan was sent to Miqodesh to seek the counsel of the Agasti in the first place."

Sir Eban was quick to respond. "A wise comment, Elderman."

"But wisdom is not going to prevent more tragedy," Haden

gruffly added. "Look, I'm a practical man. Everyone in Mortania is concerned with the same fears, but no one is willing to do what it takes to address them. Whether or not these fires were set, none of the towns seemed to have been prepared for emergencies. Any number of unexpected tragedies can crop up. In Mortinburg we have a fire response system. We have an emergency plan. Rather than hunting down something we don't understand, we need to rally all the towns of Mortania, set up a comprehensive safety plan that each town can implement, and stop these tragedies before they strike. Causes are secondary. Prevention is where our attention and limited resources need to be spent."

Finally, Waljan squeezed into the conversation. "But isn't catching the perpetrator the most efficient way of preventing further attacks, Haden? *Practically* speaking?"

"There is a difference between catching a perpetrator and chasing illusions," Haden suggested. "You heard Moriel. The real Maweth is dead. Anything else is rumor."

Mack reasserted his argument, undeterred. "Whether Maweth's death was exaggerated, or he's risen from the grave, I have been tracking him throughout Mortania for at least a year. He lurks unseen and can engulf an entire community in flame instantly. He leaves no tracks. He makes no sound.

"Many communities beyond your borders have been suffering under the senseless destruction of the Shadow for some time. You have come late to this party, friends. So forgive me if I take your assurances with skepticism. We need to stop him."

Haden challenged him. "Hold on one minute! First you say Maweth is a flesh-and-blood bad guy that you've been tracking for a year. Then you say he makes no sound and leaves no tracks. But how exactly do you track a flesh-and-blood bad guy that makes no sound and leaves no tracks, Mr. Slade? I have been a hunter since your father cut his first teeth. A hunter can only track something real. Something real has weight. It leaves prints and waste behind. You can't have it both ways. This talk of a

'Shadow' is nothing more than assigning tragedy to an imaginary villain—an attempt to personify misfortune. Sometimes people find more consolation in identifying a source for their troubles."

Mack fumed, "Troubles, you say? Misfortune? Tragedy? Troubles and misfortune are common, Mr. Hunter, and tragedies are random. Spontaneous infernos consuming one town after another like a contagious disease is neither common nor random. No, sir. Maweth is real."

"Where is your evidence?" Moriel asked testily.

Mack reached into his pocket and pulled out a linen handkerchief delicately embroidered with florals in teal, fern green, and magenta. He placed it on the table.

Culbert snickered. "So . . . the Shadow Assassin does needlepoint?" Noticing Haden's eye roll he followed his quip with an apology. "Just trying to lighten the mood."

Mack gingerly unraveled the handkerchief with the edge of a blade. A glittering red disk encircling an intricately carved heart lay in the center. "I don't dare touch it. It has dangerous properties. This is his signature. He leaves them behind with the destruction."

Sir Eban spoke up. "Waljan, did you or any of your friends find similar artifacts of this gemstone in the ruins of the Sanctuary?"

Waljan looked to Culbert and Ander for a response.

Ander just shook his head bashfully as Cully explained, "Sir, there was a lot of debris, and we were focused on finding survivors. The only precious stone I saw was the Stone of Sages—or what was left of it."

Pointing at Mack's gem, Moriel declared, "This proves nothing. Mack could have found that token at a curiosity shop in Bayside."

"A *fire gem*? In a curiosity shop?" Mack scoffed. "I'm going to ignore the fact that you've called me a liar and ask if you really think the owner of a curiosity shop wouldn't know the value of fire gems on the black market. Or that selling them would jeopardize his business. Selling fire gems is illegal in most Mortanian villages. Everyone knows that."

Haden interjected, "Regardless, Mack, they aren't called fire gems because they literally start fires. In fact, their proper name is epithymite. These gems are dangerous for the fire they ignite in one's heart. I have seen their effect on more than one person I care about. It's devastating. An all-consuming desire for something they'll never have steals the victim's good sense. Although it's disturbing that anyone is harvesting these gems, I don't see how it connects a particular person, let alone a particular myth, to a set of arson attacks."

"Besides, Mack, your honor aside, we don't know you," Moriel argued. "We can't just take your word that this is more than a piece of colored glass. Nothing illegal about selling red glass in a curiosity shop. Or a garnet, or ruby, or any number of plain red gems."

"A piece of glass? Pick it up if you are so certain I'm lying!" Mack insisted. "Should be easy enough for a guy who wears a death stone around his neck," he quipped.

Sir Eban intervened, "Mr. Slade, let me clear up some confusion for you. We do not wear *death stones* around our necks. It is merely an opal that contains certain energy properties. Those properties are not exploited for harm. The Abidanian culture controls all opal deposits in Mortania, and I can assure you they are used only for communication."

"Thank you, your honor," Mack said with a mocking bow. "Now, let me clear up some confusion for *you*. Abidanians are not as successful in controlling this substance as you might care to believe. Abidanian or otherwise, someone has found a way to weaponize them." Mack pulled his tunic off one shoulder to display a large ugly, ragged scar. Everyone in the room froze.

"It's a brand," Mack continued. "Where I come from it's given to those who have 'disrupted the social order' and are convicted to a life of slavery. The brand is made by a device that harnesses the unstable energy of what we call white gall or death stone—an opal very similar to yours. And it produces a level of pain worthy of its name—one that never lessens."

"I am very sorry for what you have endured, Mr. Slade," Eban soberly stated.

"Look," said Moriel. "I appreciate what you are trying to do here, Mack. But . . ."

"Enough!" Waljan shouted, bringing a host of disapproving eyes upon him. Sheepishly, he continued. "Mack is telling the truth, Moriel. I saw Maweth. The Shadow Assassin is real."

Moriel breathed out his frustration. Still, much of it lingered. "Wally, we know that you have an extraordinary gift for visions and insight, but a half-dream produced by a stone in a pool is not evidence. It was just a vision. It can't be relied on without other evidence."

"No, Moriel. I didn't just see him in a vision. I saw *him*. I saw Maweth in the flesh. And he saw me. I am certain of it." The moment that Waljan dreaded had finally arrived. He had to reveal why he failed to show up at Miqodesh before the attack on the Sanctuary. It was an admission of failure. Heroism and suspicion betrayed him. His willful defiance, despite good intentions, had drawn Waljan away from the Sanctuary.

Waljan explained that as he approached the outer borders of Miqodesh, he spotted a cloaked figure prowling among the undergrowth. Drawing his sword, Waljan called out the Abidanian greeting. The prowler sprang away.

Waljan admitted this was not his mission. He knew at the time that the Agasti awaited him. But he felt the circumstances warranted action. The Hero of Mortinburg was not going to allow a suspicious character to skulk around the Sanctuary without an explanation. So he pursued the figure for some time. After a while Waljan fell back. He reasoned that it would be better to track the prowler at a distance under the pretense that he'd given up the chase. It worked. The prowler led Waljan straight to Mount Sar. There, in the foothills, the chase would end abruptly.

Waljan had carefully read the forest floor when suddenly his speaking stone began to sing from deep inside his pack. The reverberation was low, like a man's voice, but it did not form words that Waljan could recognize. Befuddled, he pulled out the stone. As he examined the swirling surface, a cloth bag was thrown over his head, and Waljan was tackled to the ground.

"And that," Waljan admitted, "is how I wound up in Cloakwood, tied to a tree."

Disappointment swept through the room. Eyes like rapiers fixed on him, cutting deeply and painfully into his soul. He could not bear to return their gaze. The Agasti and the Stone might have been saved had Waljan obeyed his orders.

8

Petit Fours and Prattle

"Can we bring the meeting back to order, please?" Mrs. Pruitt caterwauled over laughter, gossip, and the tinkling of silver spoons against delicate china teacups. The library of Josephine Pruitt's spacious home was filled to capacity with a gaggle of chatty, bubbling, well-dressed ladies too engaged to notice her calls for attention. Mrs. Pruitt slammed a heavy gavel atop the mahogany desk. The members of the Mortinburg Women's League settled down.

"That's better. Now then, I would like to thank you all for coming, and especially for Polly Sweet's contribution to our treat table. The petit fours were simply delightful!" Polly's rotund cheeks flushed as she acknowledged the compliment with a quick wave.

The Mortinburg Women's League comprised the wealthiest and most idle of Mortinburg's female citizens. Founded as a charitable organization, they spent more time eating and socializing than serving the community. But they were generous with their dollars when a crisis arose, and the most recent tragedy in Smithtown provided that opportunity.

"Before we adjourn today, I have three final announcements. First, I am so delighted to present this month's Charitable Heart award to Madeline Templeton of North View, who has decided to start a Women's League chapter in her own town."

A tall, thin, timid looking woman with a birdlike face approached from the back of the room, all smiles and blushing. Josephine placed a trophy topped with a glistening heart-shaped gem in Madeline's hand. The woman drew the trophy to her chest and then suddenly grew very concerned.

"Oh my!" She said. "I have been here too long. I must go!"

"No time for a speech?" Josephine pleaded.

"No, no, no! What was I thinking? I shouldn't have even come—I have so much to get done! Thank you, Josephine. I am very proud to have received this honor. Forgive my rush." With a quick wave to the ladies and a burdened expression, Madeline collected her belongings and hurried away. The ladies were perplexed. But they excused her with cheerful congratulations.

Josephine continued undistracted, "Secondly, I am happy to report that we have met our financial goals for rebuilding Smithtown, including the installation of an honorary plaque at the Smithtown City Hall thanking the Mortinburg Women's League for our contributions to the relief and restoration effort!"

The women congratulated themselves with vigorous applause until Mrs. Pruitt raised her hand for quiet. "Lastly, could all the Abidanians in the room please stand?" A small group, including Polly Sweet, whose chubby dimpled cheeks turned as red as her smiling lips, stood with anticipation. "It is only right to especially honor the Abidanian community, who went out of their way to help with the crisis in Smithtown. I have decided, out of my own private funds, to award the Abidanians in each Mortanian town with a custom sculpture on behalf of their sisters in the league!" Josephine bubbled as she displayed an unusual globe sculpture encased in delicate, silver-cast filigree. From the center of the globe, a luminescence escaped and shimmered like stardust.

After a chorus of "oohs" and "aahs," the ladies returned to their petit fours and prattle until there was nothing more to eat nor to say. As they spilled out of the library, through the grand entryway and into the street, Chaz Myrtle fought his way in like a salmon against the current. The last Women's Leaguer cleared the foyer, and Mrs. Pruitt nearly closed the door in the poor man's face. She startled.

"Oh! Mr. Myrtle! Whatever are you doing here? Please, come in." Her voice echoed in the vast, emptied foyer.

"I'm afraid I have come with urgent news," Chaz answered as he took in the magnificence of Mrs. Pruitt's mansion. The foyer was encased in polished mahogany, cherry, and walnut, inset with geometric designs of alabaster. An ornate crystal chandelier hung from a cathedral ceiling in the center of the floor. At the back of the foyer, a sweeping staircase ascended to the second floor, flanked by a wall of paintings, mostly of Mrs. Pruitt's late son, Caddock.

Chaz noticed a number of expensive collections filling the space. Shadowboxes full of rare butterflies hung on the walls. A display of dainty gemstone figurines sent droplets of colored light about the room. And across from the large window that extended to the ceiling from the top of the front door, a grouping of rare orchids graced a small console. If the rest of the house was as glorious, Chaz felt he could spend the entire day just exploring its treasures.

Mrs. Pruitt had not lived in the home long. She had taken possession of the property formerly owned by Justice Asmodeus after he disappeared during the Battle of Centennial Court. Without any known heirs to take ownership, the judge's estate was auctioned off the following year. Josephine was among the very few that showed interest, and she snatched it up at a bargain.

"May I get you some tea, Mr. Myrtle? Assuming the ladies did not completely empty the teapots. No matter how much food I prepare for these events, it never seems to be enough!"

"No, thank you, Mrs. Pruitt. As I said, this is urgent and it concerns you directly."

"Well, then, let's have the news!" Mrs. Pruitt replied as she busily struggled with the clasp of her necklace.

"May I help you with that?" Chaz asked, hinting that he needed her full attention.

"Thank you, but no. I've got it," she replied. "Go on. What is your news?"

"It's about your son, Tyre."

"Oh?"

"No need for worry, ma'am, I'm sure. But, he's been detained at Smithtown. Some misunderstanding."

"No, Mr. Myrtle. It's no misunderstanding."

"You already knew?"

"I was there when it happened," Mrs. Pruitt said calmly. "I just returned to Mortinburg yesterday in fact. Apparently, the citizens of Smithtown have reason to believe that my son is involved in the tragedy that occurred there."

"You must be outraged! After all you have done for them."

"I'm quite sure the sheriff would not detain him without sufficient cause, Mr. Myrtle."

"But he's your son. Surely you don't think that justice is being served. You don't think he is responsible, do you?"

"I don't know what to think. Since Tyre has joined that murderous Abidan community, there's no telling what atrocities he is capable of. It certainly has nothing to do with me."

"Mrs. Pruitt. You know better than to make that accusation."

"I see they have gotten to you, too, Mr. Myrtle."

"But Mrs. Pruitt, your own husband . . ."

"Let's not speak of the dead, if you please, sir. Now, excuse me. I have an important business trip to prepare for. Thank you for dropping by."

Stunned by Mrs. Pruitt's condescending apathy, Chaz froze a moment, mouth agape, before realizing how silly he must have looked. He dismissed himself clumsily and headed to Caddock General Goods for a few supplies.

Chaz barely heard the store bells jingle as he pushed through the door and ambled over to the pig feed absentmindedly. Josiah Constance immediately took note of Chaz's puzzled expression.

"Can I help you with something, Chaz?" Mr. Constance asked.

"Nah, I just have to remember what it is I came in for." Chaz turned to the merchant and offered his hand. "How are you doing, Josiah?"

"Fine, thank you," Josiah said, chuckling. "But you seem a bit out of sorts. Unless you are intending on adding a herd of pigs to the cattle ranch, I think you are in the wrong aisle."

"Yeah. I just have a lot on my mind. Did you hear about Tyre Pruitt?"

"Afraid so. I witnessed the whole thing. I'm sure it will be all right, though. Just a lot of raw emotion out there, and understandably so. I wouldn't be too concerned."

"I'm more perplexed than concerned. Josephine seemed to be quite disinterested in her son's predicament. A worrier like her—just doesn't seem natural, does it?"

"If I had to figure out Mrs. Josephine Pruitt, Chaz, I think I would be at it indefinitely. That woman has all sorts of mystery about her."

"I suppose you're right. She certainly has been good to you, though! Investor and biggest customer, I see," Chaz said, noticing a new display of gemstone figurines just like the ones displayed at the Pruitt Estate.

"What do you mean?" Josiah asked.

"These gem figurines. Josephine has a load of 'em back at the house."

"Oh. She's been supplying me; I haven't been selling to her. They aren't the kind of thing I normally stock, but you know Josephine. She insisted I carry them. I thought if we displayed them closer to the door, they might catch the eyes of passersby. I have more floor space than I used to, but still not enough for inventory that just sits."

"Where does she get them? I never thought of Josephine as a businesswoman."

"Well, rumor is that when she bid on the Asmodeus place, she took the entire estate, furnishings and all—including the deeds to a few mines that the judge had left behind in his desk drawer when he skipped town."

"So that's where all her money is coming from!"

"Could be," Josiah replied. "But then again, she doesn't make a dime off this lot. I'm ready to give them away."

"We certainly did walk in at the right time!" exclaimed an elderly patron who had just swooped into the store with her granddaughter. Both were dressed in black, which looked particularly out of place on the curly-headed girl with sparkling eyes and pudgy pink cheeks. "We'd gladly take one off your hands!"

"Are you going to take advantage of an honest man's ill-timed remark?" Mr. Constance teased the shopper. "Tell you what—I'll throw in a free figurine with your purchase of anything else in the store. How does that sound?"

"I'm always in need of eggs and flour," the woman answered. She turned to her granddaughter. "Now, Hazel, which figurine did you want?"

"I just want Daniella back!" Hazel insisted.

"Of course, dear." The grandmother turned to Mr. Constance. "Do you have any dragon figurines?"

In an attempt to charm the little girl, Mr. Constance said, "It just so happens that lost dragons fly in here every day, hoping that clever little girls like you will take them home. I do believe one of them was calling for a Hazel this very morning."

Little Hazel glared at Mr. Constance disapprovingly. "Daniella can't talk. And she can't fly, either."

"Of course, of course. You want one of those non-flying, mute types of dragons. Okay. Let me see what we have." Mr. Constance reached into the back of the bottom display shelf and pulled out a stunning emerald green dragon dramatically poised to strike, with flaring nostrils and a gaping mouth. He presented it to the hopeful child.

"No! Daniella is a red dragon!" the child protested. "And

she has tinier wings, and longer ears and she is hugging a big red heart right here." Hazel poked her own chest with a chubby forefinger.

"I'm sorry, miss. We don't have *any* red figurines. But this one really needs a friend. Can't you see how lonely he looks?" Mr. Constance said.

"I want Daniella!" the child wailed. Her grandmother tried to calm her, but the little girl carried on so mournfully that the woman apologized and ushered little Hazel out of the store.

"Ma'am! What about your eggs?" Mr. Constance cried as the door slammed shut. He turned to Chaz, growling, "You see? This is what comes of letting Josephine make inventory decisions!"

Chaz Myrtle laughed. "Well, Josiah, how about you help me find some manly leather polish for my side saddles and some good, strong jerky? And before I forget, Moriel and Haden asked me to pick up a few things as well. I'll be meeting up with them in Smithtown."

Mr. Constance led Chaz down one aisle and then up another, taking the least efficient route to the saddle polish. Along the way, he tried to catch up on the news while periodically calling Chaz's attention to his newer products. "I haven't seen Haden in weeks. Oh! You should try this feed additive. Full of vitamins. Builds immunity against hoof-and-mouth disease. How's the old man doing, anyway?"

"He's not the strong hunter he used to be. But you couldn't tell by his ornery nature. Tough as ever, that old bird."

"Tough he is." Josiah pulled a smooth metal bar from the shelves. "Take a look at this—it's a new style of bit. Supposed to be much gentler on the horse's mouth." He handed it to Chaz and continued down the aisle and around the corner. "Maybe we can get Haden to slow down. I think clerking is a lot healthier for a man his age than traipsing through the wilderness. Isn't that the reason he moved away from Mortwood in the first place?"

"Yes, it is. But you know what they say: 'a toothless tiger is still a tiger.' The woodland is in his blood."

"Yeah, well I could use him back in the store." Josiah rang up Chaz's purchases, wrote them down in a ledger, and walked him out to the street. "I'll send you a bill for the goods. Give my regards to Moriel and tell Haden a position is waiting for him here."

"I will, Josiah, but I doubt it will do much good. Haden will die happier under a tree than under a roof," Chaz said, taking his leave.

Moriel, Waljan, and Haden rode over the plains of Mortania toward Smithtown. They planned to meet up with Chaz and see about bail for Tyre Pruitt. Sensing that Haden's steed had fallen behind, Moriel slowed his animal to a halt and glanced behind. Haden wasn't too far back but plodded slowly forward. It was clear he needed a break. Moriel swung his horse around and waved. Haden returned the gesture. Noticing that Moriel had stopped, Waljan trotted his mount back to Moriel's side.

"Let's walk the horses awhile," Moriel said. "Give Haden a chance to catch up. It'll allow us time to talk things over."

Waljan knew this was not a conversation that Moriel wanted to have. Waljan wanted it even less. He swayed with the horse's gait, patting the animal's neck and talking to him softly—anything to avoid eye contact with Moriel. The horses snorted softly and sighed. Their hooves fell in heavy thuds over the sedges and clover.

Moriel began a fatherly lecture. "There are some things, Wally, that we can understand only through experience. We make our observations, analyze a situation, and make the best decisions we can under the circumstances. But when we lack experience, it's too easy to make mistakes—grave ones. The fault doesn't lie in one's natural ability but in the lack of real-world training. And that's why obedience to one's superior is a paramount discipline."

Waljan ruminated on Moriel's words. Then he asked, "And what if, through ability or chance, we know something that someone else couldn't, despite his experience?"

"For example?" Moriel challenged.

Waljan replied, "You, with all your experience, don't have the gift of sight. You, with all your experience, were not with me the night I followed the Shadow to Mount Sar. How do you know that my own experience is insufficient under those circumstances and that yours would be enough?"

"As far as you're concerned, I don't have to know. It's my call, Waljan. You don't even know what the Shadow looks like and yet you claim to have seen him. What color are his eyes? How tall is he? Does he have a scar? A limp? A crooked smile? A large nose? Don't tell me you know who you saw!"

Moriel broke off to catch his breath and calm down. Then, quieter, he continued, "Someone is burning down villages, yes. Someone or a group of someones. But the Shadow Assassin was a uniquely powerful and insidious presence that struck panic in the hearts of Mortanians."

"You act as though you knew him," said Waljan.

"I did. And it won't help us to spread these rumors . . . to increase the fear. People become very dangerous when gripped with fear. An arsonist is a mere criminal. Maweth was a monster. Do you not see the problem? Do you not see your own arrogance?"

"Why is it arrogant to worry that you are missing something important here? Do you really believe that an Agasti master can be traumatized by a common criminal? Chen was terrified. He was barely coherent! Come on, Moriel. I need you to trust me. I know I still have a lot to learn. But I think I am right on this."

"Waljan. This is no longer up for discussion. As a Knight of the Realm you have taken a vow of obedience—to me. I have really stuck my neck out for you. Some think you were knighted too early. Why do you think they sent you on a diplomatic mission to Miqodesh? It wasn't a mission, it was an errand. They were sending Waljan the message boy, not Waljan, Knight of the Realm, Hero of Mortinburg. And well they should have because they are worried that you are too impulsive and eager for your own good. It was a test that you failed. Your fate as a knight is not in your own hands. It's in mine. And in the judgment of the Twelve."

"My fate as a knight is in the hands of the king," Waljan growled and kicked his horse into a canter, breaking away from Moriel's side.

Haden trotted up to take Waljan's place next to Moriel.

"Is he going through his Tribulation or causing yours?" Haden asked.

"I didn't see this rebellion in him initially. I'm not sure what it means."

"You saw it. But at the time you just mistook it for youth. And aren't you the one who keeps telling me that he isn't a child anymore? Maybe we need to let the reins out a bit," Haden suggested. "Mistakes are part of the learning process, after all."

"That from a man who couldn't go a day without pacing a trench in the floor, waiting for Wally to return from Cloakwood," Moriel ribbed.

"Yeah, well. I know Cloakwood," Haden replied. "Understanding the growing pains of a young man is far more complex."

"I'm worried, Haden. I don't know if I can trust him. And I must. The knights are the only ones capable of stopping this Maweth business. Provincial law enforcement aren't prepared to solve a regional problem like this. But if Waljan is going to obey his impulses above his superiors, he will be more of a liability to me than an asset."

"I don't think you need to worry," Haden replied. "He's adjusting, that's all. He's a young man trying to find his way."

"As long as he doesn't lose sight of the king's way."

9

Friends and Enemies

Tyre Pruitt shivered violently as he leaned back against the cruel cement wall of his cell. On his forehead and above his top lip, beads of sweat formed. The back of his shirt was soaked through. With every movement, his muscles groaned. And the constricted veins in his temples pounded.

The Smithtown jailhouse was built into a wooded hill, leaving a single point of entry into and out of the cells. Consequently, there were no windows, no air circulation, and little heat. All the comfort Tyre had was a thin blanket on a plank bed.

Voices echoed through the air, accompanied by vague commotion. Tyre was certain he was hallucinating when the door of the cell lobby swung open and the ghostlike images of Wally, Moriel, Chaz, and Haden came floating in. Tyre tried to speak to his vision, but the only thing he could voice was "Mmmori . . ."

"We need to find the sheriff immediately," Moriel said to his companions.

Waljan ran up to the cell door and spoke through the bars, "Tyre! We're here. We're going to get you out. Don't worry, buddy."

From around the corner, Sheriff Malvo entered the room with a tray of steaming broth and medicines. Seeing the party gathered there, he halted.

Waljan took one look at the scarred face and thick black hair and lunged at the officer. "Bruce Malvo!" he shouted. But before Waljan laid a hand on the sheriff, Moriel grabbed him by the scruff of the neck and slammed him against the opposite wall. Bo Dog scurried around Moriel's feet, barking in protest.

"I have had just about enough of your impulsiveness, Waljan!" Moriel scolded. "Now sit down, or I will throw you in the next jail cell myself!"

Stunned, Waljan sat. He sat like a small child caught stealing candy from the local grocer. But deep inside him, resentment rose in silent fury. Bo Dog, sensing his master's mood, lay his big yellow head in Waljan's lap and appeased him with puppy eyes.

"Whoa!" said the sheriff. "I nearly spilled my patient's soup! Sir Moriel, Mr. Pruitt thanks you for that intervention, I'm sure. He needs fluids *now*. Dr. Mallow just left. Now, Mr. Hunter, if you wouldn't mind, there are some blankets in that bag behind you. I think they'll make your friend a bit more comfortable. And this is Mr. Chaz Myrtle, am I right? Mr. Myrtle, could you unlock Mr. Pruitt's cell? The keys are hanging by my left pocket."

With raised eyebrows, Chaz complied with the lawman's request. Everyone in the room had previous run-ins with the leader of the Malvo gang, hired by Justice Asmodeus to police Mortinburg years ago. But now was not the time to bring up old feuds. The men worked together like a practiced triage team to get their patient comfortable, fed, and treated.

Tyre swallowed the last spoonful of broth and fell into a deep, convalescent sleep. After securing the cell, Malvo motioned the visitors out of the cell lobby and down the hall into his private office to discuss Tyre's status. But Moriel made it quite clear to Waljan to stay behind.

The sheriff closed the office door and sat at his desk, asking the other men to sit as well. The room still bore indications that Malvo had only recently inherited his position. Sheriff Haward's nameplate hung on the door, and a portrait of him and his wife was leaning up against the wall along with a box of personal items that Mrs. Haward wanted to pick up.

"We heard that the sheriff and mayor were missing. Any word?" Moriel began.

"No. I'm sorry to say that we have no news. Of course, everyone expects they were victims of the fires. It's the only explanation."

"You have our sympathies." Malvo nodded his appreciation as Moriel continued, "I must say I am as surprised as Wally to see you here, Malvo."

"I understand. The old Bruce Malvo died with his gang in the Battle of Centennial Court. You're looking at an entirely new man."

"Is your boss Asmodeus aware of that?" Haden asked.

Malvo laughed. "I wouldn't know, actually. Asmodeus is, or was, a coward, loyal to himself alone. I haven't seen nor heard of him since that day. I am the only survivor of the Malvo gang, as far as I know. And after that day I took a hard look at my life and didn't really like what I saw. I thought it best to start over in a new town."

"Question is, have you?" Chaz Myrtle asked.

"Well, now, how am I going to convince anyone of that with a few words and a smile? You're gonna have to suffer a little doubt, it seems to me."

"Forgive us our apparent lack of manners, Sheriff," Moriel apologized. "We've been on the road a bit too long. What can you tell us about Tyre's situation?"

"His illness or his charges?" the sheriff asked.

"Both."

"He was fine when I first locked him up. He hasn't slept much, and it's pretty cold here at night. Doc thinks he picked up some bug that he's too stressed to fight. He's been suffering fever for at least a day and a half. His legal troubles are certainly not helping. The kid's done nothing but show up at the wrong time among some pretty frightened and heartbroken people. He's the scapegoat. That's my sense after talking to him and witnessing the crowds the day I took him in. But there is a legitimate case mounting against him. Some evidence has been uncovered and an expensive prosecutor retained."

"What kind of evidence?" Moriel prodded.

"Personal effects on the scene and some eye witnesses." Malvo answered. "But that's all I am free to say."

"We understand," Moriel said.

"There is something very wrong with this," Haden chimed in. "There is no way Tyre had the occasion or time to participate in this tragedy, let alone the motive. He was in Mortinburg when the news broke and was on his way to enlist our help before the first relief caravan left town. His own mother led the relief effort. She should be able to vouch for him."

"Yeah, but it's also his own mother who's officially pressing charges," Malvo informed them.

Haden stiffened. "That just can't be. We can criticize Josephine for many things, but she loves her family, that's certain. Why would she do such a thing? And how? She isn't even a citizen of this town."

"Well," Malvo explained, "apparently she owns several properties here in Smithtown. Or did before the fires."

"What did the doctor have to say about Tyre's prognosis?" Moriel asked.

"He's in pretty bad shape. Doc said that Tyre should be moved to a hospital bed. But all we have after the fire is the tent, and no one will allow him in there among those still recovering. Not only is he unwelcome, but Doc is afraid he might be contagious. He's got nowhere else to go but here."

"Can you allow us to take him away for treatment on our word that we'll return him when he's well?" Moriel pleaded.

"Are you crazy? If I allow a band of Abidanians to take custody of Tyre Pruitt, this town would skin me alive. Of course, if he somehow escaped while I was off duty, I might be willing to suffer a bit of public shame." The men considered this suggestion and nodded their agreement.

Malvo took no time to set things in motion. He glanced at

the wall clock. "Well, would ya look at that! Time for me to clock out for the day. Thanks for dropping by, gentlemen."

The men followed Malvo back to the cell where Tyre slept, motionless. Waljan glared at the lawman as he grabbed his keys, unlatched the cell door, and swung it open. Then, without another word, the sheriff left the jailhouse and locked the door behind him.

"Is he letting Tyre go?" Waljan asked. No one seemed to hear him.

"Moriel, Tyre is clearly too sick to return with us to Dead Springs," Chaz said. "Don't you think we should find some place closer to take him?"

Haden chimed in, "We certainly can't take him to Mortinburg. It's the first place they'll look. It would seem that Josephine won't take him in anyway."

"We'll take him to the healers in the caverns at Eastern Ridge," Moriel said. "They'll know how to help him, and he won't be discovered there."

Waljan interjected, "He will be discovered, Moriel. The Shadow Assassin is Abidanian. He will know how to find the caverns. He may even be among our own community!"

"He won't, Waljan," Moriel replied with warning in his voice. "You need to trust me."

"But, Moriel!"

Moriel swung around and grabbed Waljan by the front of his tunic, pulling him a fraction of an inch from his face. Baring his teeth, Bo Dog snarled and barked out his objections. Haden scrambled to Wally's aid, but the old man could not free him from Moriel's grip.

Waljan felt Moriel's hot breath with each word his mentor growled. "I have heard the last of your opinions about this matter, boy. You are to follow orders and remain completely quiet, do you understand?"

Waljan couldn't help himself. "But, Moriel, I—"

"Do you understand?!" Moriel belted out.

Waljan shot his arms through the center of Moriel's grip, knocked his hands away, and pushed him back. Moriel lost his balance and hit the ground. Through fits of coughing, Haden pleaded for the tussle to stop, but Wally drew his sword and pointed it at the stunned Moriel. Everyone froze except for Haden, who was gasping for air.

"I am not your '*boy,*' Moriel. I am Waljan of the Realm, a Knight of Abidan, the Hero of Mortinburg." Embarrassed and frightened by his own anger, Waljan sheathed his sword. "I'm sorry, sir." Waljan offered Moriel a hand, but Moriel refused it. "It's just . . . what is it going to take to earn your respect?"

"More than a Spirit Sword and a moniker. You may not be *my* boy, but you are still *a* boy, and your little adventure at Miqodesh proves that. If you can't obey your superiors, you are no use to the Realm. Now go. Be a hero if that is what you want."

Haden, still coughing, sunk to his knees before Moriel, and Waljan realized how much he struggled. Wally hurried to Haden's side, but Haden put up a hand to stop him.

"I'll be all right, Wally," he wheezed. "You need to go."

Waljan felt sick. His head swam, and his vision narrowed. He wondered how this all went so badly so quickly but concluded that it had really been brewing for days, maybe longer. After a moment of indecision, he whistled for Bo Dog and disappeared with the dog into the waning light as night fell on Smithtown.

Master Chenaniah's long white whiskers flittered against his cheeks as he faced into the wind above a raging sea. Restored to his full strength, he sat cross-legged on a craggy boulder above the caverns of Dead Springs. Despite his stiffly upright posture, the old man seemed completely relaxed. His folded hands cradled a darkened, lifeless speaking stone, and his eyes were closed in meditation.

With feet bared, Penelope approached as softly as a kitten and folded up on a ledge just below the master. She dangled one leg toward the sea below. The chatter of gulls rose above the ocean's ebbing roar. Bursting in all directions and falling back into a churning mass, the waves broke against the rocks, sending up a fine spray to wet Penelope's toes.

"What do you seek, my child?" Master Chen asked, eyes closed like a statue come to life.

"Purpose," Penelope answered. "Peace. A place."

"It is all one and the same," said Chen. "When you find your purpose, you will find peace in knowing your place in the world. Then, no matter where you are, you are where you are supposed to be. And then you are home."

Penelope looked up at this paragon of quiet assurance. Chen was eternal wisdom trapped in finite frailty. But despite his tissue-paper skin and snow-white mane, he seemed more vigorous now than a man half his age. She marveled at his ability to weather the sadness of life.

"But, Master Chen, don't you feel lonely? Disconnected? Your friends are gone. Your home destroyed. Your entire life has been turned upside down! How do you recover from that?"

"I am not alone, Penelope. Even now I am with my brothers, with the family of Abidan, with my king. We are all connected. Always connected, in life and in death. For death is just an illusion."

"I don't understand. My mother and father died a long time ago. If their absence is just an illusion, then why have I missed them so much for so long? What kind of cruel game is perception, if my parents are really here but I can't see them, talk to them, or be with them? And how much can I trust what I experience?"

"Why do you assume that reality is only what you sense?" Master Chen asked. "Tell me, do your senses perceive the drama of sea life unfolding before us, just below the surface of this great ocean? Predators larger than any animal on land roam, their shimmering prey darting and zipping nervously about. Others simply float in large communities, feeding off of whatever nutritious material passes by. All manner of strange creatures undulate, crawl, and burrow. They illuminate, camouflage, migrate, and build. Do you witness any of it?"

"Of course not," Penelope replied.

"But it unfolds just the same," Chen said. "We see the sunshine glint off the surface. The waves gently ebb and flow, rise and tumble into foam. And a universe lies hidden beneath. I admit that our senses are a powerful distraction from hidden realities. But those realities touch us more deeply than we know. Mastering our senses is like parting the waters to experience life beneath the surface. Come, sit and close your eyes."

Penelope obeyed. Chen offered a wrinkled hand and she took it.

"Now take a few deep breaths. Empty the cares from your mind. What do you see?" he asked.

"Nothing."

"What do you feel?"

"Warmth? Calm? I don't know . . . maybe nothing."

"Ah, yes," Master Chen chuckled. "She does have a stubborn streak." Chen carried on in a one-sided conversation as if Penelope weren't even there. "Yes. I think you are right about that," he mumbled. "Ah . . . well, we will see."

Who is he talking to? Penelope thought. She couldn't tell if he was teasing her or losing his faculties.

Finally, Chen opened his eyes and said, "Nava sends you her regards."

Penelope smiled wryly. He was playing with her, surely. She wasn't gullible. "Sir Chen, I may be young, but I have seen enough for three lifetimes. I am not so naïve."

"No. You are not naïve. You are a warrior. You are a servant-heart. You are the daughter of Patrick and Merilee Longbow. And you are greatly loved."

Tears stung Penelope's eyes at the sound of her parents' names. "You knew my parents, Master Chen? I didn't tell you their names."

"I did not know them, child. But I do know them now. They are here with us."

"What? Where? How!" Disbelief and desire slammed together in Penelope's heart. She had lost her parents at such an impressionable age. Through dreams, memory, and longing, it was easy to have entertained fantasies that they had not in fact died but were just gone for a time and would return. But now, as a young woman she should know better. The conflict between mature, cold reason and childish delusion tore at her soul.

"Where are they?" Master Chen repeated back to her. He took Penelope's hand and placed it over her heart. "They are here. And on the other side of Castle Wall, hoping you will join them."

"But how do you know this?"

"The Agasti have an enhanced sense of the Realm. Most Abidanians require the speaking stone to communicate beyond the Wall."

"Teach me to use the stone, Master Chen. *Please.*"

"Without the Stone of Sages, I am afraid that is impossible."

"I don't suppose the Stone can be repaired somehow," said Penelope.

"Oh, no, no, no," Chen replied. His wispy beard flitted from side to side as he shook his head. "Once a sagestone of that size is shattered, it becomes a potentially volatile and dangerous material. It cannot be repaired." Chen looked out to sea. "But it may possibly be replaced. I just don't know. I am only one, now."

"Master, with me you are two. With Cully you're three. With the Slade Brothers and their crew—you are many."

Chen looked at Penelope with a twinkle in his eye. "You are a very special young lady, Penelope Longbow. I have stayed in Dead Springs long enough. I think we are all ready for a journey."

10
The Core Problem

The thick earthy air weighed heavily on the miners who passed buckets of rock, hand over hand, up toward the light. There, rubble tumbled down a growing pile of discarded material. Men and women spent their days caked in a fine dust that crusted over with each day's heat. Once a week, they would squeeze under the "waterfall," a chute of draining wastewater, just to free themselves of the muck for a few hours. They clamored for a turn with heads down and mouths tightly closed to avoid the risk of illness.

Oppressive as the volcanic heat of Mount Sar, the never-ending chime of hammer-on-chisel-on-rock competed with shouts and groans and general commotion. The noise was punctuated by earsplitting blasts that spit gravel and dust through the corridors of the mine. Danger was ever present, but they were careful to avoid tragic accidents. Everyone worked in hope of freedom; they could not afford to be careless.

Belowground, teams of two squeezed into twisted passage-ways like earthworms. Squinting, each held an oil lantern against the rock walls, reading the surface for signs of epithymite veins. Deposits of ash, silica, and carbon stacked up in layers within the igneous rock. Like roads on a map, the deposits led the miners to the most productive sections for extracting gems.

Odie Cluny and Tephra Sparks vowed to remain together until both had fully satisfied their commitments and earned their release. Each miner in the field agreed to work until a particular goal was achieved for Core Mining Company. In return, they would receive their heart's desire. A contract between the mine and its workers outlined the specifics for each individual. But it seemed that as the earth shifted under the miners' feet, so did the terms of their contracts.

Odie had come from a distant land, kidnapped by a band of pirates. He had been working this mine for well over three years. He knew the layout well and had managed to befriend most of the overseers to the extent that friendship could be fostered in them. Scrappy and strong for his average frame, with wavy brown hair and olive skin, Odie looked like a storybook hero.

Tephra had arrived a year after Odie. After studying geology, she was lured away from home by a handsome gentleman who promised her a job in minerals. This was not the opportunity she had imagined. But here in the mine, Tephra and Odie met and vowed to keep each other accountable to hope.

An air horn signaled the end of the work day. Everyone came to the surface and lined up for roll call. After the workers were counted off, they returned to their cells for rest and rations of clean water, bread, and dried dates. It was just enough to keep the workers productive without causing too much trouble.

Although, most in the mines had no interest in causing the company trouble. Even with all the pain and drudgery, many saw their commitment as an opportunity to better themselves. At the very least they believed they would be adequately compensated.

Around their necks, workers wore the company insignia—a heart-shaped epithymite gem. The company motto was posted throughout the mine to remind them of their motivation: *"Core Mining Company is 'heart' at work to make your dreams come true!"* The executives had even devised a song for workers to sing at the beginning of each day.

Still, the work conditions and boredom demoralized some

laborers enough to cause discord and competition among them. Grudges and tension occasionally ended in fistfights and punishment. Every once in a while, chronic trouble-makers would vanish. At first, the workers assumed that the company couldn't afford to keep troublemakers around and simply let them out of their contract. But when disgruntled miners started to cause trouble just to get released, rumors circulated. All kinds of frightening stories passed among them in whispers.

Morning began as the workday ended, with an abrupt and brash alarm piped into each cellblock. Just an hour before one morning alarm, Tephra had finally found that place of deliciously deep sleep after a fitful night. Her body jumped obediently out of bed, but her mind was still on the cot. A bracing splash of water from her rations pail did nothing to reduce the swelling in her sleepy eyes or force them open. Pulling on her crusty boots and grabbing her leather-covered iron helmet, she waited for the cell bars to unlock and then walked down the hallway to the stair-well. Just ten flights and she would be in the fresh air.

Tephra searched for her partner, and finding him energetic and well rested she huffed, "I hope you got enough rest for the two of us."

Odie shushed her as the site manager arrived for roll call. When the workers were counted, a bugler began the introduc-tion to the Core anthem. All the workers sang.

Core Mining!
    We're heart at work to make your dreams come true!
Core Mining!
    We free the rock and build our futures, too.
We offer allegiance, proud. Our hearts all beat as one.
To finish the work at hand until that work is done.
Core Mining! Core Mining!
Let us work to the core for the Core!

At the final refrain, the people were dismissed to their day's labor.

"Now, what were you saying, Tephra?" Odie asked as they made their way to their assignment.

"You may be carrying some of my load today. Rough night."

"I would happily carry some load for you, partner," Odie said with an assuring pat on Tephra's back. "Anything to get us out of here before they change the terms on us again."

"Oh no, now what?" Tephra asked, anticipating the newest injustice.

"Well, I'm not sure, but look who's raking up over at the rubble pile."

"Patterson? She was supposed to be released yesterday! What is she still doing here?"

"I'm going to guess she missed some fine print written in her contract or didn't quite understand the terms of her agreement . . . something like that anyway."

"She was so excited to see her children. She must be heartbroken. It's so unfair. It's always something! Odie, do you know anyone who has left here after satisfying their commitment?"

"The only ones I've seen leave have been carried out. And that's not the way I plan to go."

"What if that is the *only* way to go?" Teph worried.

"What about Manard Dawes? He's living his dream after a mere nineteen months in this place. Core has been very good to him."

"That's the story. But have you ever met Manard Dawes?"

As was his habit, Odie played nervously with the gem that hung low on his chest. Then, with renewed desire he said, "I'm gonna finish my work, collect the land deeds I was promised, and make my way to the open country. Come on. We have work to do."

Determined to double his output by finding untapped veins of epithymite, Odie worked his way as deep as possible into his assigned shaft, descending seventy feet into darkness. Tephra followed close behind. Staying together was the best way to fight the daily struggle against a range of conditions. The darkness was so black, it seemed to ooze right through them. Disorientation was a constant threat, and getting stuck in a tight place could be deadly.

Odie found a good spot to begin extracting gems and set to work while Tephra set up the pulley system that delivered the product to the surface. After about two hours of hard effort, Odie was struck by panic. It was a reaction he suffered several times during a single work day. With little room to move, the desire to escape intensified. Odie's heart pounded against his sternum and he started to hyperventilate.

Tephra sensed the coming terror and took over. Gifted with a soothing voice, she was golden at times like these. She began humming softly. Just as they had practiced so many times before, Odie matched his breathing to Tephra's seraphic tones. As her voice climbed the scale, Odie breathed in. As she descended, Odie breathed out. Then she began to talk him through his fear.

"I am safe. The mountain protects me. I'm relaxed, the mountain supports me. I am well. The mountain provides." They repeated their mantra together until Odie's calm was fully restored.

"Thank you, my friend. That was a bad one," he said.

"It's the least I can do for someone who offered to take up my load," Tephra replied warmly.

Deep in the rock, as if coming from a different world, a heavy rumble vibrated.

Odie shook his head. "That was a doozy! I didn't know they were blasting today."

"They must have brought in a new supply of white gall," Tephra answered as she clipped a bag of ore to the rope and inched it up the shaft.

Another rumble resounded through the mountain, this time bringing down slivers and chunks of stone around the two miners. Wide-eyed, Tephra looked to Odie for assurance.

"It's fine. We're okay," he told her. It was a curious feature of Odie's personality that panic set in when all was going well, but in a crisis he had nerves of steel. The partners were opposite in that regard, one of the many ways that made them a reliable team.

Odie placed his chisel to a crease in the rock and chipped away. Suddenly, a low sustained resonance grumbled from the depths. "That better be your stomach, Teph. Please tell me you missed breakfast."

"We don't get breakfast, Odie," Tephra quipped wryly, trying to make light of what she suspected was a dangerous situation. The vibrations grew more violent until the tunnel began to shake and then lurch. "Quake!" Tephra screamed.

"Surface! Surface! Go!" Odie yelled back.

Tephra snaked her way up the shaft, flung about by the quake and making little progress. Odie was knocked farther downward. He could hear the tunnel cracking and crumbling higher up. Sharp bits of rock flicked his face and ricocheted off his hard hat.

"Tephra!" Odie shouted against the maelstrom. He scrambled in her direction but had no traction, and was swallowed up by the mountain, tumbling and rolling deeper until freefalling several feet into a sloshing pool of hot sulphur-laden water. Struggling against the force of erratic and unpredictable waves, Odie thrashed about, trying to stay above water and avoid slamming against protrusions of rock. Finally, the mountain settled.

Battered and nearly drowned, Odie chose a direction and swam until he could feel a ledge. Coughing up water, he pulled himself over the ledge and rolled onto his stomach. When he woke and remembered where he was, Odie noticed that enough light was present to see the perimeter of the chamber. He listened. A distant roar told him that water escaped the mountain. If water escaped, perhaps he could as well. Returning to the mine the way he came would be impossible.

But then Odie realized he had no desire to return to the mine. He reached for his heart gem. It was gone. He thought of Tephra. He doubted she survived but couldn't dwell on her.

It was too difficult. *I have to get out of here while I still have strength,* he thought.

The light brightened slightly. Odie reasoned that the sun must have shifted and would likely move away just as quickly. He had to get moving. He could swim out but would be at the mercy of the current if the pool led to a waterfall. He decided to shimmy along a narrow ledge and follow the flow.

As Odie went along he said to himself, "I am safe. The mountain protects me. I'm relaxed, the mountain supports me. I am well. The mountain provides. I am lost but the mountain leads me. I am sad but the mountain consoles." Over and over he repeated this refrain until he reached the open air. With a twinge in the pit of his stomach, he approached the ledge where the water tumbled out of view, hoping for a drop he could survive. To his astonishment, the water cascaded down a stepped config- uration of rocks along a gently sloping trail. He simply walked away, free and unharmed, hoping against the odds that Tephra had similar luck.

11

Daniella

Chaz Myrtle dismounted and tied his horse to one of the trees that lined South Court Way, right in front of the Pruitt mansion. Indigestion gurgled in his stomach at the thought of addressing Josephine about her son for a second time. But it couldn't be helped. It was the decent thing to do.

He rapped the goat-head knocker against its bronze base and listened for movement on the other side. The handle jiggled, and the door cracked open slightly.

"You again?" Josephine asked, peeking through.

"Yes, ma'am. I'm afraid the situation with your son has changed," Chaz responded.

"They aren't releasing him, are they?

"No, ma'am."

"Well?" Josephine replied impatiently. "If you've come to say something, say it and let me get on with my day."

Chaz stood there, silently pleading for a more welcoming reception. This was not the kind of news he wanted to deliver through a slit in the door.

Mrs. Pruitt sighed heavily. "Fine, then! Come in. I suppose you would like a cup of tea?" she said, more out of habit than hospitality.

"No, ma'am," Chaz replied as he stepped over the threshold and into the foyer. He removed his fedora and proceeded to mangle the rim nervously. "Moriel wanted to come himself, but . . ."

"Just as well. I have little patience for that man."

"Josephine," Chaz said. "Tyre is very ill."

For a moment, Mrs. Pruitt stiffened with parted lips. Her eyes widened. But the expression passed as quickly as it had formed. "How ill?" she asked as if mildly curious.

"Enough that Doc can't tell us anything one way or the other. He may recover. He may not."

"Well, that is very inconvenient. What good is a doctor who doesn't know his profession?"

"Moriel is trying some of his ancient remedies. But we are not even sure what Tyre suffers from. He must have picked up some kind of virus, but the doctor thinks that emotional stress is worsening his condition."

"So I suppose you want some compensation for the doctor? Is that why you are here?" Mrs. Pruitt's voice became tight and harsh.

Chaz did not understand the cold belligerence he faced. Josephine had always been so delighted in her boys. He could not conceive of anything that Tyre could have done to cause such a rift between them. "No . . . ma'am . . . I just . . . I thought . . ." He struggled for words that should not have needed to be said.

"Very well. Stay here," she replied abruptly and rushed out of the room.

Chaz tossed his hands in the air and began walking in circles. Women always threw him off-kilter. Chaz Myrtle, one of Mortinburg's more successful ranchers, never married. He found much more in common with his cattle than with female humans. But Josephine Pruitt took the prize. Never would he have imagined such a callous reaction. Minutes passed. Chaz slapped his fedora against his chaps, wondering whether she'd gotten lost in her own sprawling home.

He meandered over to one of the display cases he had

noticed on his last visit. A menagerie of figurines glittered in the expansive, well-lit entryway. A crystalline pony reared up gracefully and pawed the air, his mane flying up like waves on a stormy sea. On another shelf, a delicate rose-quartz bud lay as if lazily cast aside by a fickle schoolgirl. Next to it, a plump, ebony beetle squatted stubbornly, facing off a fiery red dragon with wings unfurled and ready to soar.

Daniella? Chaz couldn't figure why that name came to mind. Listening for Mrs. Pruitt, lost among her many rooms, Chaz opened the display case and extracted the dragon. Instantly, like an electric jolt, he was hit by a bottomless loneliness and pining he'd never experienced in his life. The dragon slipped from his fingers and onto the marble floor, losing a wing on impact.

"Well, here you are," Mrs. Pruitt said as she hustled back into the foyer. "I am sorry I kept you wai—" She stopped mid-word when her eyes fell upon the little broken dragon. "Ever try admiring with your eyes, rather than your hands, Mr. Myrtle?"

Chaz felt like he'd lost three feet of height. "I am so sorry, Josephine. That was very clumsy of me."

"You're not half as sorry as the little girl who owns that dragon will be," Josephine remarked. Without the slightest difficulty or expressed emotion, Josephine picked up the dragon and its wing and returned them to the case. "I guess the homes of unmarried ranchers are not typically stocked with precious art and finery." Mrs. Pruitt held out a thickly stuffed envelope. "This is to be regarded as a charitable donation to the doctor from the Women's League for his work with the poor invalids of Smithtown. Is that understood?"

"Yes, ma'am, thank you." Chaz adjusted his fedora firmly on his head and slunk out the door like a shamed dog. The embarrassment of his forward and clumsy mistake forced Chaz to replay his behavior at the Pruitt mansion over and over in his mind. Then it came to him. Daniella. A little girl. The little girl in Josiah's store! Daniella was the name of the dragon figurine she was searching for. But there was something very wrong about it all.

Chaz returned to Eastern Ridge Falls, where Moriel sat grinding medicinal weeds into a fibrous pulp. Tyre's fever had raged through the night. He mumbled his way through hallucinations and nightmares, reliving his childhood and inventing new worlds full of insurmountable dangers and paralyzing fears. He writhed in his sleep. By the time Moriel ventured above ground to collect feverbud and wiltweed, Tyre had fallen into a heavy slumber.

"Is Josephine coming?" Moriel asked.

"No. But she sends her regards in the form of gold," Chaz replied, tossing the envelope of banknotes on the ground next to Moriel's mortar and pestle.

"She can't see that Tyre suffers as much as she does from the past, and he deserves it far less," Moriel complained.

"I have a feeling she has more to suffer yet," Chaz said.

"You didn't have to take the money, you know," Moriel suggested.

"She caught me off-guard. I was distracted. I—"

"Morieeeehhh . . . Moriel . . ." A sleepy voice drifted up from the cavern below the falls.

"Our patient awakes! This is good. It looks like I got this paste ready just in time!" The good knight scooped up his medicinal and the envelope and waved for Chaz to follow. "We can chat below."

They passed through the stony archway into the cavern and down into the healing cove, where Tyre sat up on his cot, rubbing his hands over his stubbled face.

"Well, this stuff works miracles!" Moriel said cheerfully. "I haven't even given you any and you're better already."

"If you call this better you're a lousy healer, Moriel. I feel like someone stuffed me in a bag, hung me from a tree, and beat me like a dusty rug for three days."

"It was actually just two days, but I was trying to get in a good workout," Chaz teased.

"You had us really worried, kid," Moriel added.

Tyre looked around. He ran his fingers through his thin, sandy hair and scrunched up his face as if trying to remember something important. "This isn't Dead Springs."

"We're back at the falls," Moriel replied. "You haven't been in Dead Springs for weeks."

"I can't distinguish my memories from those crazy fever dreams," Tyre explained. "Moriel, were you and Haden dancing the Huk Tah with the Banna people in a fertility ritual?"

"That would have been the crazy fever dream," Chaz offered.

"Yeah, right," Tyre replied. "And being thrown in jail by Bruce Malvo?"

"No, that actually happened," Moriel said.

"Ugh. Maybe I should just go back to sleep," Tyre concluded as he flopped back onto his pillow.

"Before you do that, let's get some of this paste into you and a little food. You're not out of the woods yet."

Chaz sat down at the foot of Tyre's bed as Moriel administered his concoction. "I saw your mother today, Tyre."

"Did she disinherit me yet?"

"This rift between the two of you isn't new, is it?"

Tyre shook his head as he grimaced with a mouthful of pulverized wiltweed. He swallowed hard and gagged. "Ugh! Seriously Moriel? I'd rather die than take another dose of that stuff!"

"Well, that could be arranged," Moriel teased.

"So, what did you want with Mom?" Tyre asked Chaz.

"We just thought she should know about your condition. What exactly is going on between you?"

"You know that Dad was Abidanian, right? That he died in service of the king?" Tyre began. Moriel collected his medications and left the room. "Well, she has never really gotten over that. And she still believes that Wally was responsible for Caddock's death. It's not too difficult to see how she might resent Abidanians and the king for the loss of her family. My joining the community must seem like a betrayal. I can't blame her, really."

"So why did you join?" Chaz asked.

"Because if I had to choose between Mom on this side of the Wall for a short time, or Dad on the other for all eternity, well, you can see which is the better choice. I love my mother. But I love my dad, too, even though I've never met him. And if there is a chance I can convince Mom to come with me to Abidan, then everyone wins."

"You are wise for your years, Tyre," Chaz said. "Get some rest. Moriel and I need to go into town."

Chaz and Moriel left Tyre in the capable hands of Abidanian nurses to rejoin Haden on the top floor of Geezer's Geyser, a tavern in the center of Mortinburg. The Council of Twelve had called a meeting there to address the Shadow and other issues. Having always been a hotbed of Abidanian activity, the Geyser was bequeathed to the council on the death of its original proprietor, Gerald Guest. It remained open to serve the Mortinburg community, but also provided a reliable location for council meetings. A large portrait of "Geez" hung over the dining area's mantle.

"What could be keeping Haden?" Moriel murmured as the meeting carried into its second hour.

"He's got to be here, somewhere. He told you he would be, didn't he?"

"Not in so many words, but I did expect him. He'll show up. By the way, wasn't there something you wanted to tell me back at the cavern? Something to do with Josephine?"

"Oh, yes!" Chaz remembered. "What would you think about gifting a fire gem to a little five-year-old girl?"

Moriel's eyes squinted sternly. "What are you talking about, Chaz?"

"Josiah and I were talking in the store a few weeks ago, and a little girl came in with her grandmother. They were looking to replace a dragon figurine that she had lost. I found it at Mrs. Pruitt's."

"Josephine stole a little girl's dragon figurine?" Moriel asked, confused.

"I don't know how Josephine got it, but that isn't important. It's not just a glass bobble. It's a fire gem," Chaz explained.

"How do you know?" Moriel asked.

"I picked it up, and it was like nothing I have ever felt before. Like a waking nightmare," Chaz said with a shudder.

Someone in the room slammed a fist on a table and grumbled about why Wally had missed this year's Harvest Festival. For a moment Chaz and Moriel took note of the argument that followed and then returned to their hushed discussion.

"What makes you think it was the little girl's dragon? There must be more than one dragon figurine in Mortania."

"Josephine told me it belonged to a little girl. Whether that little girl was the one I met or not, no child should possess a fire gem. They're illegal for a reason."

"Of course. It is very odd," Moriel admitted.

A woman in the back of the room carried on, shrieking out complaints and poking the air with her index finger.

"But odder still, Moriel, after I dropped the dragon, Josephine picked it up like it was nothing special. Just returned it to the shelf as if it had no power over her."

Moriel sat up in his chair and seemed to disappear within himself. He was drawn out by more raucous debate and scanned the crowd once more for Haden. Sir Allred tried to calm the assembly with his gavel.

"Maybe it's better that the hothead *isn't* here," Chaz said, raising his voice against the increasing clamor around them. "He'd be hacking and spewing and interjecting through the entire meeting. It's contentious enough as it is."

"Good point. I didn't expect this to get so heated," Moriel admitted. "Still, it's not like him to miss a council."

"He's pretty upset about Wally," Chaz reminded him.

"I know. We got into a pretty good argument about that yesterday, and he hasn't talked to me since. I understand his worry, but Wally is a young man now, and Haden doesn't seem to recognize that."

"And you do?" Chaz replied.

"You think I don't?" Moriel asked.

"I can't know that. All I know is that you treat him differently than you do me or Culbert Longbow or Mack Slade. You evaluate his choices, monitor his actions, correct his errors."

"You three are not Knights of the Realm. You haven't accepted a vow of obedience under my training. Yes, I worry about Wally. But for different reasons than Haden does."

"Moriel, regardless of his vows, Wally needs the self-assurance that he can stand on his own—not just with a bow or a sword, or his wilderness skills—but with his decisions. He already second-guesses himself. In his position, I would crave your trust more than your correction. I still don't understand what happened between you two back at Smithtown. It seems to me that Wally is more competition than apprentice."

A proud man would have argued the point. But Moriel knew that Chaz was an honest observer. He couldn't dismiss his impression out of hand. "If that is how it looks to you, Chaz, I will have to consider my motivations. You're a good man."

Chaz nodded in appreciation. "So, what do we do about Josephine and this fire gem?"

"I am not sure right now. Let's talk to Haden about it. He may have good input."

Moriel and Chaz turned their attention toward the proceedings, which now addressed Waljan's failure to follow through on his mission and to protect the Sanctuary.

"Perhaps we have put too much pressure on the boy. He was given more responsibility than he is ready for," said one of the elders.

"Waljan of the Realm has more heroism in a single strand of his hair than you old cronies have in your entire self-important bodies!" snipped a supporter to a chorus of "Yeah!" and "Hear, hear!"

"Why don't we let him speak for himself? Where is the Hero of Mortinburg?" asked Allred. "Moriel?"

Moriel stood with apprehension. "I am not certain where Wally is at this time. We parted at Smithtown." He sat down.

Sir Allred persisted. "And where did you send him? What is his destination?"

Moriel stood again, this time more slowly. "He needed some time away, sir. For reflection." Chaz shifted in his chair.

Sir Allred nodded in acknowledgment. "Very well."

An attendee chimed in, "Why are you council elders focusing on Waljan when we have another Abidanian—or someone passing as one—roaming the countryside wreaking havoc and mayhem? Do you realize what rumors are flying around? That Maweth has returned and that we are responsible?"

"Yeah!" said a young merchant. "I was stopped on the road to Bayside yesterday. A gang of northeasterners noticed my speaking stone and accused me of being a Maweth follower. They set my rig on fire and would have done worse if a group of kind strangers hadn't come by just in time. I am tired of taking the blame for this evil!"

"Now, now, gentlemen . . . ladies. Let's not get carried away," Sir Allred said in a calming but tired manner.

"Maybe the Shadow Assassin *is* an Abidanian," said a woman from the back of the room. "Why do we always assume we are so much better than anyone else?"

"And maybe *you* are just a loon! Or maybe an agent of Uriel?" screeched yet another in reply.

The meeting further dissolved in a flood of accusations and counteraccusations. Chaz and Moriel settled in with their arms folded and their jaws set. It was going to be a very long night.

12
Strange Encounters

Bo Dog howled mournfully to Waljan's lament.

Weep, weep! How the wounds run deep,
Hidden streams of crimson tears
Stain my soul, I am swallowed whole
And in triumph, malice nears.
My many faults have claimed me.
The unjust judge has named me
No one else can blame me more than I.

"Yeah, you're right," Waljan admitted to his whimpering companion. "It's a pretty morbid song. But if anything is going to put me to sleep tonight it's a brooding ballad. And I don't want to stare at these stars all night long."

Waljan lay on a bed of fallen leaves, moss, and decaying cedar pulp under a heavy woolen blanket. He caressed Bo Dog's wiry head and fondled his velvety ears. The day's events ran through his mind over and over, torturing him for his lack of self-control. *How do I fix this?* he thought.

Bo Dog grunted, whined, and rolled over for belly scratches. Waljan obliged and praised him for his loyalty. "I thought you were going to tear Moriel's leg right off, boy. You can be pretty threatening when you want to be."

Bo Dog sighed with deep satisfaction at his master's approval. Suddenly, he pricked his ears and jolted up with a whine. Waljan reached slowly and silently for his sword and rolled out from under the blanket onto his stomach.

"Bo Dog, drop!" he commanded as he reached for his canteen and emptied it on the fire. Waljan gently swept his arm along the ground, dumping moist debris over the smoldering embers and then topped them with his blanket to suppress the smoke.

Raising himself silently into a crouch, Waljan listened hard. Bo Dog whined again. With a hand over the dog's muzzle, Waljan whispered consolations. "Shhh, it's okay, boy."

A light burst from inside Waljan's pack. It was the speaking stone, humming as it had on Mount Sar. All the muscles in Waljan's body released their tension, and he breathed easily once again. He removed the stone from the pack and placed it in his lap. It spoke.

"Waljan of Abidan, Knight of the Realm," said the voice. "I weep."

Waljan looked up. Before him stood a beautiful vision—the Queen Mother of Abidan. She was clear in his mind but not in his sight. Vibrant colors and intense beauty came to him as thought, while his eyes saw only a grayish-white apparition. The more he focused his eyes on the sight, the more it seemed to fade.

"Why do you weep, My Lady?" he asked her.

"Do *you* not weep, my son? What you suffer, I suffer. What I suffer, the king suffers. Why do you invite suffering? Is there not enough to contend with from without?"

"I do what I think is right, My Lady. But it turns on me. I am weak. Foolish."

"Your thoughts reveal reason without truth. Your spirit feels your mind's deceit. You are neither weak nor foolish. You are willful."

Shame overtook him. "Yes, My Lady. I am. I should have obeyed Moriel at Miqodesh."

"Why did you not?"

"I thought my decision was a better one. I thought I had more insight and that it would override Moriel's judgment."

"And would you override the king's judgment on the strength of your insight?"

"Of course not, My Lady!"

"It is one and the same, my son. It is the king to whom Moriel answers on your behalf."

"I assumed he would agree," Waljan explained. The Queen Mother folded her hands before her. Waljan's thoughts blossomed as she waited. "I had no right to that assumption, did I?"

"I know you meant well. But do you think the king was ignorant of the threats against Miqodesh? Just as a small child cannot fully understand the dangers from which his father protects him, neither you nor Moriel can fully comprehend the directives of the king. But the king knows the strengths and weaknesses within you both. By refusing the proper order and discipline, you have caused more suffering than was needed— suffering you were sent to prevent. We obey because we do not have the ability to see all ends."

"I knew the moment I stepped into the Sanctuary that I might have helped the Agasti escape," Waljan admitted. "And I have been trying to set it right myself. But alone, I am not enough."

"You understand. That is good. Now I give you a new mission. Will you question my orders as you questioned your Mortanian master's?"

"No, My Lady. You have my word."

She shook her head in sad concession. "So much pain made worse by the struggle to avoid it. People refuse to see. It is only through suffering that love blooms to its fullest. But we can suffer too much—most often by our refusal to suffer at all." The vision began to dissipate into darkness as the Queen Mother said, "Trust."

"And . . . what is my mission, My Lady?" Waljan asked as the vision ended.

The queen's final word lingered momentarily as Waljan startled awake and threw off his blanket. Bo Dog slept quietly beside the glowing embers about which a low flame still flickered. A light fog wound through the trees, diffusing the moonlight. Waljan located his speaking stone and tested it. Still dead.

Just another dream, he thought. But it didn't matter, either way. He was still expelled from the company of his closest friends, unsure of what to do next. It seemed that the dream might have given some direction but ended too soon. The more he tried to recall the details, the more they evaporated from his mind.

After steeping a warm cup of pine needle tea, Waljan sat, allowing his brain to adjust to wakefulness. He massaged the sleep from his neck and shoulders. As the bluish-gray of dawn crept up from behind the trees, the fog lifted. All but a handful of stars had faded.

It was the perfect time of day to hunt down a small doe or nab a handful of rabbits for breakfast. But after an hour of stalking the woods, he and Bo Dog settled on a cache of boiled quail eggs and wild mushrooms. When he'd finished eating, washing, and packing, Waljan retrieved a small, ornate crystal bottle filled with clear liquid. He poured the water into a bowl set before him. Then Waljan began to sing the Misting Chant.

The bards are mute, the songs unsung
But you are not forgotten.
The waters hum, "Dear children, come,
The king waits in the mist!"
So gather in, our joys begin
The king waits in the mist!

Swirling and twisting, ribbons of vapor snaked from the bowl and formed a cloud around Waljan. He extended his arms and surrendered to the mist. It was in this mist that Waljan had first encountered the King of Abidan in a manner that set him apart from other Abidanians, even among the knighthood. As if by special invitation, Waljan was offered a glimpse of the kingdom he longed to enter, the kingdom that occupied the lands beyond Castle Wall. The people of Mortania could see the peaks of Castle Mount, jutting high above the earth, but no living soul had ascended them.

Waljan hadn't ever had another vision like that since his first Mist Rite at the Eastern Ridge Falls. Being known as having the "gift of sight" was an embarrassment for its exaggeration. He tried to keep that first vision in memory, but as time went on, it seemed more the product of a daydream. It was difficult not to question its authenticity, especially now. As he completed the ritual, he could only trust that his king received him in the mist, offering peace, forgiveness, and strength.

"Well, Bo Dog," he said to his eager companion, "I suppose I can just leave it up to you. We can rejoin Peep and Cully at Dead Springs, wait for this flap to blow over at our old hangout by Castle Wall, or wander the forest aimlessly. What'll it be?"

The yellow lab barked as he backed away from Waljan toward Dead Springs, beckoning him with droopy brown eyes. Waljan laughed at the dog's response.

"I swear, Bo Dog, sometimes I really think you understand me. Okay, on to Dead Springs. Let's see what Peep and Cully have been up to while we've been gone."

At Waljan's approach, Bo Dog leapt a one-eighty and bounded ahead, always keeping just in sight of his master. The autumn colors radiated with the early morning sun, lending an illusion of warmth to the chill. Waljan would hike a good day and a half before arriving at the inn the following afternoon. He spent the hours puzzling over the bizarre events of the previous weeks.

Haphazardly setting fires to peaceful villages violated everything an Abidanian believed. Waljan realized that Moriel must be right—there was no mysterious Abidanian villain. Maweth was history and legend. His vision at the sea must have been a confused jumble.

But then, he wondered what good was the Stone of Sages, or any lesser speaking stone, if they communicated confusion rather than truth? Had he, for example, ever really seen the king? Had he ever truly spoken to those beyond Castle Wall in the Realm of Abidan? Or were these just illusions induced by some trick of the mind? Waljan's purpose—his very existence—hung on the reality of Abidan. Now he doubted all that defined him: his identity, his mission, even his relationships.

Bo Dog stopped, tense and alert, and raised his nose to the air. His ears flitted like antennae. A fat squirrel vaulted from the trunk of a sugar maple. Barking hysterically, the dog took off, chasing the poor creature in, out, and around the underbrush.

"Bo!" Waljan yelled, running after him. But Bo Dog skipped out of sight. "Stupid dog!" he complained as he slowed to a halt.

"You have a fine animal, there," came a voice.

In an instant Waljan, sword drawn and poised to strike, faced the man.

Without the slightest flinch, the man said with soothing calm, "You can lower your weapon. I'm unarmed."

Waljan slowly sheathed his sword, his eyes trained on the stranger.

"The dog's a retriever?"

Waljan tried to excuse himself from conversation. "Forgive me, sir, but I have a long journey ahead and a dog to find."

"Of course! Of course! I'll walk with you. Carry on. Name's Bart, by the way."

"Waljan Woodland," Waljan replied with a curt nod as he forged ahead in search of Bo Dog.

"A rather ordinary name for someone wielding such a beautifully adorned sword," Bart observed, matching Waljan's pace.

"I acquired the name before I acquired the sword," Waljan said and whistled for Bo Dog, hoping the man would take the hint and leave Waljan to his search.

"And what do you call her?"

Waljan corrected him. "Bo Dog is a male."

"Oh, no . . . I meant your sword," said Bart.

"Ah . . . Bergdis," Waljan said.

The man nodded. "Did you train Bo Dog, or was he trained when you bought him?"

"Neither," Waljan replied. "I found him in a shallow frog pond by my childhood home, barely weaned and nearly drowned. I guess you can say we trained each other, if you consider running off after a squirrel *trained*. And he isn't for sale, if that is what you are suggesting."

"I have no need for a hunting dog. But I do admire quality when I see it."

"Are you from Smithtown? Or traveling?" Waljan asked before calling for Bo Dog again.

The man searched his thoughts and then replied, "I'd say traveling."

Waljan snickered. "You'd *say*? That's a curious way to phrase it."

"I suppose I am a curious sort of person," Bart replied.

Waljan nodded and pushed on, hoping the man would lose interest. There was too much on his mind to engage in idle, useless chatter, especially with the added distraction of losing Bo Dog. But Bart kept up energetically.

"Now, this is real living, don't you think? The earth beneath your feet, the crisp, cobalt, autumn sky overhead, a fine companion at your side—or ahead of you as the case may be." Bart breathed deeply. "This is real! This is reliable."

"Ye-up," Waljan answered, struggling with his patience.

"And then again, maybe not?"

Waljan turned toward the man, about to respond, but no one was there. He wheeled around and flinched at the site of Bart calmly strolling on the opposite side.

"Your problem, Wally, is that you are living with one foot in this world and one foot in the Realm. You have to make a decision," Bart said.

Waljan halted. "It's *Waljan*. And what are you talking about?"

"One can't serve two masters. You can serve the king, or you can serve your pride. But you can't do both. An army that fights itself loses even when it wins. It's important that you return to your people at Eastern Ridge."

"And what would you know about *my people* or Eastern Ridge or me, for that matter?"

"You are Waljan of Realm, are you not? Eastern Ridge Falls is the location of Mortinburg's Gathering, where the Abidanians go to perform the Mist Rite. Your people are the Abidanians of Mortinburg, but more specifically Haden Hunter and Moriel of the Realm. Should I continue or are you satisfied?"

Waljan stared hard at the man. There was nothing remarkable about him; he was an ordinary, middle-aged man. But he had a bit of mischief in his eye, the kind that Waljan used to see in the expressions of Tyre and Caddock Pruitt just before they set up a prank or when they shared an inside joke. That look made Waljan uneasy. Suspicious.

"The last time I met someone who knew more about me than seemed appropriate, the meeting nearly led to my imminent demise. That doesn't tend to promote trust in strangers. Did Moriel send you? Or is this some kind of trick?"

The man laughed warmly. "Oh my, Wally! This is no trick. It is important that you return. That is all I can tell you."

Bart's geniality had Waljan second-guessing himself. "Why should I return? They don't want me there. Moriel and Haden were pretty clear about that. Moriel doesn't recognize that I am more than a confused kid, stumbling over my own naïve decisions."

"And you do? Sounds to me like you want to convince yourself as much as them," Bart said in a fatherly tone.

"Look, I hate to be rude, but I really don't have time for this," Waljan huffed. "Bo! Come!"

"All right, Wally. It's obvious you don't believe me. Let me help you. You are on your way to Dead Springs to meet up with Penelope and Culbert Longbow. By the time you arrive, they will no longer be there. They are returning to Miqodesh."

"I don't know what you're up to, Mister . . . Bart . . . whoever you are. But you know too much about me and my friends. A malevolence lurks in Mortania that no one understands. You could be part of it. Are you a friend? Are you a foe? I can't tell."

The man handed Waljan a leather neck pouch with the initials "BP" embroidered in the center. "Present this to Moriel. And *trust*."

Suddenly, Bo Dog pushed through a large clump of fern and pounced on Wally from behind. He barked and whined in apologetic euphoria. Waljan bent down briefly to greet the dog with mild rebukes, and then straightened to interrogate Bart further. But the man had taken his leave as quietly as he had come. Waljan shook his head and continued on his journey, scolding Bo Dog as they went.

In the hours that followed, Waljan articulated for himself the many reasons Bart could not be trusted. But either way, Waljan couldn't entertain Bart's suggestion. He was tired of being tethered. Hadn't he been obedient to Moriel through the years? Hadn't he been loyal to the king and an effective representative of the Realm? It would be reasonable to expect a little respect and independence. Who told Moriel when and where to go? Who commanded Haden? Moriel wouldn't dream of disrespecting Haden by ordering him around. It seemed to Waljan that he had earned his equality among them. He had grown up, and they simply didn't see it. His thoughts carried him out of the wilderness and over one final bluff to the grassy plain that sloped down to his destination.

Had Dead Springs been lonely before, it was now virtually abandoned. A white-haired woman with a slight hunch and twisted, bony fingers fumbled with the sheets that had been drying in the wind. Recognizing the last place he saw his friends Cully and Peep, Bo Dog whined plaintively, staring at Waljan with pleading eyes.

"Okay, you old mutt. Go get Peep!" Waljan said.

Bo Dog raced ahead toward the inn. Waljan followed, calling a greeting from a distance. The old woman looked, then returned back to the laundry as if his greeting was the random, far-off cry of a wild animal.

As Waljan neared, the woman didn't bother to face him but kept at her chore, saying, "Room 4 is open. I will make up the bed when I am done here, but you will have to fetch your own water basin. And that dog stays outside. I just mopped the floors."

"I am actually here to meet with my friends. Master Chenaniah of Miqodesh and Penelope Longbow."

"No one here but you and a traveling salesman in Room 1."

Waljan's stomach lurched. "Do you know when they left?"

"I'm just here for the cleaning. The clerk will return shortly. You wouldn't happen to be that Wally fellow, would ya?"

"Yes, I go by Wally," he replied eagerly. "Is there a message?"

"An envelope—on the buffet table," she replied without the slightest pause in her work. The woman gathered her clothespins and the basket of sheets and hobbled up the porch stairs, adding, "You staying or leaving?"

"Staying for now, I guess," Waljan yelled back as the woman disappeared through the open door.

Bo Dog found the water trough in no time, so Waljan left him to his blissful draft and went searching for the buffet table. Retrieving the envelope from the table, he sat down and opened it.

Wally—
With Chen, on way to Miqodesh with Slades.
~ Peep

The lurch in his stomach had swelled into a general nausea. How could Bart have known this? There was no mention of him in the note. Abidanians populated every town in Mortania, and

Waljan enjoyed a certain notoriety among them all. Bart could know quite a bit about Waljan without ever having met him. But knowing the Longbows, their relationship to Waljan, *and* their current plans was impossible unless he had actually been here and interacted with them. Self-doubt flooded Waljan's mind. Frozen with indecision, he decided to eat, rest, and make plans in the morning.

13

Rope and Rumors

"You have a lot of pluck for an old codger, Chen!" Mack said jauntily. Ander wished he could disappear for the embarrassment of it. He always had a more refined way about him than his brothers and didn't understand their blindness to Master Chen's unique and superior dignity. "Codger" was, without question, an inappropriate descriptor. Still, Ander realized that this was Mack's attempt at respect.

Master Chen noticed Ander's beet-red ears and retorted gaily, "Well, that is what they called me back in my youth, you know. 'Pluck.' I was small and wiry, but I could wrestle a wild boar. No fear!" He winked at Ander as he led the troop around large swaths of brambles, down shadowy, verdant corridors, between rock walls, and up rugged slopes toward Shroud Peak.

"I still can't believe you made this trip on a stretcher! This is rough terrain," Mack exclaimed.

"Well we couldn't have done it without Ander," said Penelope.

Mack scoffed. "Is that so?"

Penelope stopped in her tracks. She turned and glared at Mack. "How long were you tied up in Cloakwood, Mr. Slade?"

Mack snarled, "What's your point, lassie?"

"How long were you helplessly and hopelessly restrained after we left you in Cloakwood? And who freed you? Think about that before you mock your little brother."

"Yeah? Well everything that kid knows he picked up from *me*," Mack grunted sheepishly, strutting past Penelope.

The travelers ascended a ridge that lead precipitously to the cliffs of Whispering Gorge. There, an ancient suspension bridge spanned the ravine, providing a little-known shortcut to Miqodesh. The bridge had been too precarious to bear Master Chen and his stretcher during their earlier journey to Dead Springs. Now that Chen was able to walk on his own, the party was relieved to learn they would make record time on this trip.

"Sir Chenaniah," Ander said, "I don't understand why you want to return to the Sanctuary."

"Well, that's not surprising coming from someone who's lived a nomadic life," Master Chen responded. "But I think even a nomad can experience the sanctity of place. In all your travels, did you ever encounter a setting to which you seemed to belong? A place that appealed to you not only in beauty, or utility or community, but in a manner that bonded you to it? A place you would not have wanted to leave—the only place to which the word *home* would truly apply?"

"No, sir. I never have," Ander replied. "But I'd like to."

"Perhaps someday you will. A ruin it may now be, but Miqodesh is my home. Even more so, it's my sacred purpose."

"I don't know what you mean," said Ander.

Chen nodded. "This mountain range is rich in many valuable resources. Some of those resources have powerful uses, some dangerous. Some are highly desired, some quite mysterious. For example, to the south lies Mount Sar, which contains rich veins of epithymite, or fire gem. They are very difficult to mine, though many people have suffered the attempt. The stone has strange properties and has been known to cause emotional instability—even insanity in rare cases. Some people believe it holds the power to free men from the concerns of life. Others, that it has the power to enslave. Imagination, intrigue, and scarcity have made epithymite valuable contraband.

"Then, ahead of us, Shroud Peak holds Mortania's primary deposit of sagestone, the opal from which we carve our speaking stones. To us, sagestone is sacred. It allows us to connect to the Realm and to each other. It's the Agasti mission to protect that unity. And that is why I must return. It won't be long now. The bridge starts just beyond this bend."

The party cleared a row of trees, and a deep ravine sunk down before them. Where Chen expected a bridge, he found nothing but an enormous gap. Pounded deep into the earth and buttressed by stone, two posts stood like sentinels. The frayed remains of broken rope flapped in the wind. Barely visible against the opposing cliff, the splintered remains of the old footbridge dangled.

"This is an unexpected and unfortunate turn," said Master Chen.

"There must be another route," Mack responded.

"There is," Chen answered. "It will add another day, I'm afraid. And I hope no one here is squeamish. There is a switchback trail cut into the cliff face. It is steep and treacherous. You must take care to keep your footing."

"But then what?" Penelope asked. "We'd still have to cross the river when we get down there."

"We can wade across," said Mack.

"I don't think so," said Chen. "The water is low this time of year, but deceptively calm. The undercurrent is swift and heavy enough to push a man over, let alone a youth like Ander, or a fossil like me."

"I have an idea," Ander said. "We can lash a raft together. If Peep can shoot a line across to one of the trees on the opposite bank, we can use it like a cable ferry."

"You mean, pull the raft along, hand over hand!" said Penelope. "That's brilliant, Ander. Unfortunately, I don't think we have the right kind of rope for that. We would need something lightweight and flexible but strong. All we have is jute."

"There is a village upriver where we might be able to trade for a finer-grade rope. Do we have anything of value?" Master Chenaniah asked. The party searched their pockets and packs and came up with a few things they could part with: a couple of flint lighters, a dull knife with a mother-of-pearl handle, a bottle of foul-smelling elixir, a string of clay beads, a mosaic cannister of burial spice, and an intricately carved bone hair comb.

"Is that it? Anyone have anything else they can give up?" Culbert rallied. "Mack, I didn't see you contribute anything."

"The only thing of value I've been carrying was left back in Dead Springs. And it's most valuable to the wrong sorts of people," Mack replied. "I wouldn't trade it even if I still had it."

"Okay, then," said Culbert. "This will have to do. Let's find out what we can get for it."

After descending the narrow cliff trail and following the river north, the company came to Housh, a busy little village that seemed little more than a trading post. Plank rafts laden with goods for sale lay halfway on the bank and halfway bobbing in the water. Other vessels scraped against the muddy pebbles as their captains shoved off to carry provisions to villages downriver. Bickering over prices and quality, merchants huddled together, and little children ran about chasing chickens and tripping up their elders. The jangle of human interaction was carried off on the stiff wind.

A traveling band that included an aged monk, a redheaded huntress, and a gang of thuggish bounty hunters must have seemed an unlikely association to the people of Housh. Many interrupted their business to gawk at the strangers. Mack, who was practiced in the art of being unnoticed, suggested that the group split up. News traveled fast down the river, and it was certain that the specter of Maweth haunted the town's collective imagination.

Penelope, Ander, and Master Chen searched out a shady resting spot while Culbert and Mack hunted for a rope vendor. The rest of the Slade gang disappeared among the crowds, promising to be gone only a short time. These places always provided a diversion from the bounty hunters' hard, transient lifestyle.

Fenek trailed behind the gang like an oversized puppy, exploring the vendor tents. He loved things that tickled his senses—pungent aromas, sparkling color, curious sounds. Stopping to eye every trinket, handle every tool, and even feed peanuts to a caged monkey, Fenek lagged. Ike Slade and the crew pressed him to keep up.

Focusing his attention straight ahead, Fenek spotted a pile of coiled rope among a large cache of goods. He surveyed the crowds for Mack but couldn't find him anywhere. As he approached the vendor, a case of fine, retractable blades stole all his attention. Within seconds Fenek completely forgot what he stopped for.

"They are pretty nice, aren't they?" the salesman asked. He leaned against the case and flashed a crooked smile of gold-filled teeth. A greasy strand of his stringy hair fell over one eye.

"Yeah. I bet they's really sharp," Fenek said.

"Oooh! I imagine about as sharp as you, sir! I can tell you know quality when you see it."

Fenek giggled like a little boy but sounded more like a sleepy grizzly bear. "Yeah. But I already gots a sharp knife. In fact, I gots two of 'em. I like knives."

"Well, I have something I bet you don't have!" the man continued. "I wouldn't show these to anybody—only the most sensible and discriminating of my customers." Fenek grinned with pride as the merchant pulled out a hidden drawer filled with dainty, ceramic thimbles. They were graced with tiny butterflies, paisleys, and gilding. "Now, here is something that would absolutely delight the ladies in your life!"

A flush of deep scarlet traveled up the sides of Fenek's neck, over his ears, and around to his cheeks. "I ain't got no ladies," he said.

The vendor's saccharine expression fell. "I guess that's not a great surprise." Then, a sinister spark ignited in his eyes, and he pulled out a metal cannister filled with a putrid smelling black powder. In a hushed tone he said, "I'm sure a man like you could use a bit of this, no? It'll put a real *bang* in a late-night celebration and makes a great diversion when you need one."

Fenek shook his head vigorously and tried to remember what it was he did need. Dropping behind the counter for a moment, the vendor returned holding a black box as if it were a pigeon struggling to escape his grip. "Now, this is something you will rarely encounter." He cautiously glanced over his shoulder. "A shard from an ancient Abidanian death stone, a powerful relic from a bygone era! Would you like to see it?"

"Fenek! There you are! Ike is looking all over for you. Did you find some rope?" Mack asked as he approached the booth.

"That's it!" Fenek cried out triumphantly. "Rope! Yeah, he's got rope all right and just about anything else in the world a guy might need."

Mack patted Fenek's stony shoulder. "Good work, you big lug. Now get back to the rest of the gang. They've rejoined the girl and the old man. I'm gonna get what we need here and be on my way." Fenek trudged away as the vendor hauled a variety of rope onto the counter and Mack began negotiating.

"I'll take the comb, the beads, and the cannister," the vendor said. "But it's not going to cover the cost of that large coil, I'm afraid. Don't you have anything else you can part with?" the man asked Mack.

"This is everything," Mack replied. "Take it or I'll have to find someone who will."

"Ack, it'll do," the vendor said in a disagreeable tone.

Mack slung the rope over his shoulder and was on his way with a polite nod. He returned to the spot where Chen and the others waited and walked headlong into a heated debate. A woman, recognizing Master Chenaniah as an Agasti, had asked very publicly for his blessing over her infant. But the rumors that had traveled downriver from other parts of Mortania had grown and begun to take hold.

"Are you an Abidanian, old man?" someone jeered. "Why don't you go climb Castle Wall—no one wants your kind around!"

"You fanatics are crazy, just like your leader, Maweth!" said another.

"Maybe he *is* Maweth!" suggested a third.

But Master Chen had no shortage of defenders in the crowd now swelling around him and his party. The town of Housh, having grown up directly beneath the Sanctuary at Miqodesh, had a general appreciation for the wise men who had always occupied it. Voices of support cried out from among the throng.

"Leave him alone! He is causing no harm."

"The Agasti of Miqodesh have always been good neighbors!"

"They were victims of the Shadow Assassin themselves! You should be ashamed—don't you know what this man has suffered?"

The passions between supporters and detractors bubbled up like a waking volcano and erupted. Penelope grabbed Master Chenaniah by his shoulders and led him swiftly out of the center of flying fists and grappling bodies. The Slade brothers, who were always ready for a bracing fight, jumped into it with enthusiasm, except for poor Ander. He dodged under a hewn log bench to wait it out.

Desperately trying to quell the frenzy, Culbert stayed on the fringes, urging the ruffians to quit. It didn't help. An arm came out from the writhing mass of humanity, grabbed Culbert by the collar, and pulled him in.

14
Father and Friend

A green haze with glints of piercing light came in and out of focus above Haden's head. That, with the pressure between his shoulder blades and the damp chill surrounding him, indicated that he was lying on his back in the woods. He couldn't remember how he got there.

A horse screamed frantically amid the ruffle and snap of thrashing bushes. Haden looked around. Above him he could see a grade leading to what he suspected was a road. Slowly, the old hunter regained his bearings and made sense of his predicament. He and his entire rig had somehow driven off the road and down a steep embankment. He was trapped beneath the rig. Calling out to his frightened horse, Haden was overcome in a fit of coughing and gasping. The horse bolted hard against her restraints.

Oh, Haden, you old fool, he thought. *What have you gotten yourself into?*

Twisting his head as far as he could, he caught a vague glimpse of the whimpering animal out of the corner of his eye. She seemed to be uninjured but tangled in brush by reins and the broken shaft to which she was still harnessed. Haden cleared his throat and tried again to speak. Only a whisper came, but the horse's hearing was keen enough.

"Whoa, Bella. You're okay. It's okay," he comforted. The mare wagged her head and then settled down.

Testing his limbs, Haden managed to wiggle his fingers and then flex his wrists. A sharp, prickly sensation traveled up his arms. But at least they could move. That was a good sign. He just needed to get his circulation going.

Once feeling returned to his arms, Haden tried to drag himself out from under the rig, but his hands kept slipping in the moist debris of old leaves and pine needles. He tried to reach the saplings that grew behind his head, hoping to pull himself out that way, but they were too far away. With all the strength the old man could muster, he placed his hands against the rig and pushed. Nothing budged.

A thick branch lay just at the edge of Haden's reach. Extending his fingers as far out as possible, he walked the branch closer with his fingertips until he could finally grasp it. He pulled it above him, took the branch in both hands, and wedged one end into a small gap under the rig. Laying the branch across a large rock at his left, Haden wrapped his left arm around the extension and grabbed his left wrist with his right hand. With all his upper body weight, he pulled down hard. The rig budged an inch or two, but there wasn't enough leverage. Head swimming with the effort, he tried again. This time, the stress was too great, and the branch snapped, dropping the rig back down onto Haden's legs. For the moment, he was glad it caused no additional pain. The pounding in his head was hard enough.

"Well, I guess this is no time for pride," Haden reasoned. "But I know I'll never hear the end of it from Moriel!" He opened the small leather pouch that hung around his neck and extracted a speaking stone small enough to hide in one palm. Rubbing it with his thumb, he sung prayerfully. But to Haden's dismay, the stone remained dark. Then he remembered Miqodesh.

Haden now realized that rescue would only come by chance.

Surveying the debris that covered the forest floor, he spotted several stones, about the size of his palm, and began collecting them. Even if someone did walk or ride by on the road, he didn't have the lungs to shout for help. Perhaps a lobbed stone would get someone's attention.

Hours trudged by. All he could do was wait and think. He thought of the last time he saw Wally—angry, worried, lost in pride. Tears wetted Haden's face. In desperation, he spoke as loudly as he could, "My King, if you or your many ears can hear me, I have been an impatient, grumpy old stooge. I have left Wally to struggle alone. I am ready to enter the Realm; but please don't let me climb Castle Wall before letting Wally know how proud I am of him and how sorry I am that I couldn't have been a real father."

But then a comforting thought filled his mind. Haden *had* been a real father. He could have walked away from the infant in the forest. He could have treated the child like property—like a personal slave. Instead, Haden chose to give Wally a home. To raise him into the decent man he had become. To love him.

Haden worked a nail out of the side of his rig and found a slab of loose bark on the ground. He scratched a few words into the underside of the bark. Then, exhausted by effort and emotion, he drifted off to sleep.

Roused by the growing rumble of hooves and wheels, Haden recalled his situation. He vaguely heard a *Whoa!* and the thunderous noise came to a halt among whinnies, huffs, and moans. Fighting his heavy eyelids, he tried to look up to the road. He barely made out the bleary shape of a man in black who dismounted his horse. Behind him, another figure on horseback waited in front of a train of heavy wagons packed with human cargo. The man approached the first car and hit it hard with a stick, threatening those within to be quiet. Then, he moved to the edge of the road, looking down on the wrecked rig. Haden fell in and out of wakefulness, picking up bits and pieces of conversation.

"Why, yes, there is someone down there. He's dead, though.

I'm sure of it," the man said.

In a half-dream Haden cried out, "Help me!" But his words were heard in his own mind alone. He tried again. "Please! I'm trapped!" But only a slight, breathy moan escaped his lips.

"I think I heard him whisper something," a woman said. "Shouldn't we do something?" Her voice seemed familiarly uptight to Haden.

"All you heard were the pathetic complaints of our cargo. I'm not going to ruin a good suit to save a man who, if not dead, will be soon enough. Are you really that stupid?"

"Well, dear, there is no reason to be nasty. Just because I have an instinct for charity."

"An instinct that is not only exceedingly dull but stubborn as well. We're wasting time here."

Haden groped pitifully for the pile of rocks he had collected and, finding it, grabbed one. By this time the man and woman were settling into their saddles. Groggily, Haden tried to throw the stone toward the road. But it traveled far short of its mark and popped against a boulder, skipped downhill, and settled far below Haden.

"What was that?" the woman screeched.

"Probably the wolves coming for an easy meal," the man replied. "Let's go. I don't want a predator to spook the horses." The man gave a signal to the drivers and led the wagon train away.

Like a dream, the rumbling wagons faded into the distance, and Haden was overcome by black silence.

Penelope launched an arrow across the river and watched it miss its target several times before she successfully compensated for the added weight of rope. Finally, the soaring projectile spun vigorously around a low branch. She tugged hard. It held.

Cully and Ander had worked most of the morning lashing together the logs that the Slade brothers and their crew collected and cut to size. As soon as they had strung the throw-rope through large wooden grommets on either end of the raft, they were ready to test Ander's idea.

Having spent her childhood in the rivers of Mortwood, Penelope was the strongest swimmer of the company. She made the first attempt at crossing the river. For extra security, she tied a loop from her belt to the line. The men set the raft down in the rippling shallows and steadied it. Careful to spread her weight evenly for balance, Penelope crawled onto the platform. She grabbed the rope. The men gently pushed the craft away as Penelope pulled the main line through the grommets and slowly and awkwardly bobbed out toward the middle of the flow. Then she pulled herself back to shore.

"It's clumsy, but I think it'll work," she said on her return. "We can cross in three runs."

Master Chen, Penelope, Ander, and Ike crossed first. Then, using a retrieving line, Mack drew the raft back to the Housh side and loaded up his crew for the second run. He and Fenek embarked for the last trip over. Untying the throw-rope from its mooring, Mack instructed Fenek to sit low. But no matter how low Fenek tried to go, his bulk would not distribute sufficiently for the tiny craft. Mack tried to maintain balance as he pulled the raft to the opposite bank. With every tilt and jolt of the raft, Fenek would reflexively startle, flinch, or pop up his head, pitching the raft tumultuously.

"Stay down!" Mack commanded as he tightened his grip on the ropes. But it was too late. Fenek tumbled off the raft and drenched Mack with a wall of water as he broke the river's surface and disappeared beneath it. "Fenek!" Mack yelled. Looking on, the crew gasped. But their worst fears were quickly relieved.

The massive Fenek gained his footing and stood up. With a little effort, he staggered against the current to the bank, arriving soon after Mack and the raft. "I don't know what the big deal is. I coulda just walked across in the first place."

Mack released the raft and watched it bob and slosh

downriver as he collected the rope. After their tussle in the village, he wanted to be sure no one could follow them. Master Chen located the ancient trail that the Agasti used before the footbridge replaced it. It was surprisingly intact, kept relatively free of overgrowth by the deer, bear, and other wildlife that continued to use it.

At a slow, meditative pace, the team followed Chen up the side of the cliff. But they were in no mood to hurry anyway. During the brawl in Housh, Ike had twisted his ankle and was now limping. Cully sported a large bruise around his left eye. Mack was sore all over. Even Ander suffered four smashed fingers, trampled despite his having taken cover.

Chen and Penelope had little sympathy. They figured the men's lack of self-control might have ended much worse. As it was, their minor injuries kept them quiet and sullen. This suited Penelope and Master Chenaniah quite nicely, allowing them to walk for hours in peace.

But that peace was abruptly shattered by a burst of light that streaked above the treetops. In the distance, a thunderous boom rumbled away. Fighting his stiffness, Mack hurried his pace to reach a switchback where the trees parted. He glanced northeast across the canyon. There, from the canyon floor, a wisp of black cloud snaked toward the sky, increasingly chased by billowing white plumes. Ike caught up, followed by the rest of the group. They all stood, staring in silence as deafening as the explosion, moments before.

"Do you think that came from Housh?" Penelope asked frantically.

"I don't think it could have come from anywhere else, Peep," Culbert answered.

"It's him." Mack said. "He's struck again."

"Yeah," said Ander. "It seems we left just in time."

"We should have left sooner."

"What do you mean, Mack?" Penelope asked.

"We made quite a scene down there. Not that I regret

defending you, Chen. But the circumstances will look pretty suspicious for those who associate the Shadow with Abidan. They knew where we were headed."

"Worse, yet," Cully suggested, "Whoever is behind these attacks knows that Chen is still alive. And perhaps that he's returning to the Sanctuary."

"With the bridge out, the attacker may be deterred," Mack reasoned.

"Let him come," Peep said. "Let them all come! They'll meet my arrows before they set a single toe in that Sanctuary!"

Master Chen interjected. "Calm, my friends. Whatever that cloud signals is unknown to us—its nature, its source, its consequences. We don't know whether that explosion was intentional, or accidental. We don't know whether a single individual was injured. More importantly, it is out of our hands. Let us set our minds to the task before us."

The travelers returned to the trail and trudged up the cliff-side even more slowly than before. Chen tried to entertain them with stories of the Abidanian heroes of old. Penelope had just finished reading the story of Nava, the Servant-Heart, and was eager for more. So Chen recounted the legend of General Tsoor, who rode with the king into his final battle. When the king surrendered to Uriel, Tsoor escaped with the king's mount, Regal, riding for days until he and the horse could go no farther. He hid in the desert and bred fine steeds, all descendants of Regal. He would later sacrifice his life in service to Abidan. And then Chen told the story of Delilah, a beautiful and vain noblewoman who was disfigured by a terrible skin disease. Rather than despair, she used her wealth to care for sick and abandoned children. But Penelope was most intrigued by the legend of Anan Halak, who could pass through the mist pool in and out of Abidan, as if through a physical portal.

The team pressed on as the sun slipped below the trees and the sky above turned pale green, then apricot, then bright fuchsia. Colors bled from the sky into twilight. Weary to their core, the fellowship finally entered the Sanctuary under a black star-strewn sky.

The darkness mercifully obscured the chaos that still remained since the Shadow's attack. Jar fragments, bedding, books, and furnishings still littered the grounds. Master Chen retired directly to his small hut, which was the only space in the Sanctuary inhabited by order. Exhausted, the rest huddled around the firepit Cully had dug during their first visit. They decided to rise early and clear away the rest of the debris before Master Chen woke in the morning.

15
All Due Respect

A dense marine fog greeted Waljan as he ventured out of the Dead Springs Inn with his morning coffee. Bo Dog seemed excited at the change in weather, as if they'd magically transported to an unexplored frontier. Everything looked different under a blanket of mist. Waljan reacted with less enthusiasm. Colder days lay ahead.

A good night's rest made one thing clear: Waljan had no discernable direction. At midday, he and Bo Dog sought out Sir Eban at the caverns of Dead Springs.

"Waljan of the Realm!" Sir Eban greeted him with urgency. "I am so relieved to see you back in Dead Springs. Are Haden and Moriel with you?"

Waljan shifted his feet and stammered, "Oh, well . . . no. I think they are back in Mortinburg."

Eban's brow furrowed. "You *think*? Something unsettling has happened," he concluded.

The concerns Waljan had been shouldering gushed forth like a geyser. "Moriel and I have had a falling out. It nearly came to blows."

"Moriel doesn't often allow things to come to blows. It usually doesn't work out well for the other party."

"Yes, I know." Wally rocked from one foot to the other, working at his hands as if they were stained with bad memories. "I have completely lost his confidence and I am not sure how. He has been unusually agitated. Moody. He loses his temper. Yes, I pushed back. Yes, I disagreed with him. But he is not being reasonable."

"You are not at luxury to decide whether or not your mentor is reasonable."

"With all due respect, sir . . ."

"With all *due* respect?" Sir Eban's eyes locked onto Waljan's like a laser beam. "Waljan. How much respect is that, after all?" Waljan's face reddened with the words. Sir Eban asked sharply, "Why are you here?"

"Because I need counsel. I need guidance."

"Precisely. I am not here asking *you* for counsel. Moriel is not here asking you for counsel. You are here asking *me* for counsel—because you are not ready to discern your path on your own. And that is my point. You do not qualify the respect you owe your mentors—whether it is or is not due. You are a knight solely on their authority. The king has vested this authority in those who are properly disposed. To defy your mentors is to defy the king."

Waljan slumped onto a stool of stalagmite.

"My dear boy. You have heart, and courage, and an important role to play for the Realm. There will be time for questions and debating—for sorting yourself out. But right now we need you to see your duties through. You must return to Mortinburg as soon as possible. The threats to Mortania increase daily. No one is safe until we stop these senseless attacks. We must find the culprit and bring it to justice."

"What do you mean *it*?" Waljan asked, drawn out of his humiliation by the intensity of Eban's speech.

"We don't know who or *what* we are dealing with. A person? A group of people? A phenomenon?" Eban replied flatly. "I have had word of three simultaneous attacks in Sea Lake, North View, and Housh. All destroyed by fire. People missing. It would suggest we are not dealing with a single perpetrator."

"Housh?" Waljan asked with a flutter in his stomach. "Sir Eban, Housh is at the bottom of Whispering Gorge by Miqodesh. Peep and the others are at the Sanctuary! I must go and see that they are safe!"

"No. Your *path* is to Mortinburg," Sir Eban replied.

"But sir, please!"

"What did you think *Tribulation* meant when you accepted your knighthood? It means to suffer your responsibility. It means to trust the king, even when it is difficult to do. Do you want to continue your road blindly, or are you willing to submit your will to a greater good?"

"They are my friends, Sir Eban. They are like family," Wally explained.

Sir Eban's countenance softened. "Yes, I know, Waljan. We are all family, all of Abidan—those who have gone before and those who remain. Can a man really pick and choose whom among his loved ones should be saved and whom should be lost?"

"I don't understand," said Wally.

"You cannot protect everyone. In fact, working against the wishes of the king, a Knight of the Realm cannot protect *anyone*. You must trust him. He loves them, too. The victory of one is the victory of all. The suffering of one is the suffering of all. And the suffering will only continue if we do not stop what may be coming."

"What is coming?"

"The end. The end of Mortania," Sir Eban said with all the gravity his words implied. "I believe I have discovered the secret of Maweth. We must get word to Moriel. Now, follow me. We have a water transport that will take you directly to Castle Mount."

"Sir Eban, with all due . . ." Waljan caught himself. "Excuse me, sir. The riverbeds of Dead Springs are dry. How will we travel by water? A sea voyage will take longer than horseback."

"There are other ways. Come."

Sir Eban lead Waljan toward the back of the cavern and

through a small corridor of stone that seemed to narrow as it descended below sea level. Waljan's chest tightened, and his breath came in shallow gasps as they squeezed through a fissure and into a large expanse. The ceiling of this chamber must have been at least a hundred feet, and the sound of rushing water echoed throughout. Ahead of them stood a dock by which a crystal stream flowed. As if Waljan and Eban were expected, a man stood on the dock at attention. He held the line of a small barge, prepared to shove off.

"There are many legends and myths about the Abidanians of Dead Springs. Many claim that we enchanted the rivers to flow underground, leaving dry beds in their place aboveground."

"Hence, the name," Waljan surmised.

"Yes. Even though these networks have enabled us to survive in the face of persecution, they ran long before we arrived and have nothing to do with the drought above. This stream is part of a subterranean river system that will take you to Eastern Ridge caverns." Sir Eban handed Waljan a leather envelope. "Take this message to Moriel and the Twelve of Mortinburg. It will explain everything. May you travel in the protection of the king."

"Thank you, sir," Waljan replied as he stepped onto the craft. Bo Dog followed and settled into the hull with a whimper.

The boatman hopped next to Waljan and stored the line in the bow as Sir Eban pushed the barge away from the dock and into the current. With a long quant pole, the boatman pushed the barge against the current, driving it forward.

"I can't imagine this will be faster than a horse," Wally mumbled to himself loud enough for the boatman to hear.

"I don't know any horse strong enough to swim all the way to Castle Mount," he responded dryly.

With his gaze locked on the boatman, Wally tried to decide whether he was joking. But the man kept attending to his pole as if he'd said nothing. With smooth and steady motion, he plunged the pole deep to the river bottom, pushed the boat forward, drew up the pole, and returned it toward the bow in mesmerizing repetition. It lulled Waljan into a daydream.

The man piped up, "This course runs beneath the heart of the Crescent mountain range, northwest to Castle Mount. There are no peaks to climb. No stars to locate. No predators to avoid."

Wally was too lost in thought to respond.

"Of course," the boatman continued casually, "we should keep our eyes out for those venomous troll rats."

Wally snapped out of his silent reverie. "Venomous troll rats?"

The man laughed. "So you did hear me! There will be plenty of time for meditation, Sir Waljan. We have a long trip ahead. I like to plump the pillows before I lie down, know what I mean?"

"Not at all," Waljan replied abruptly, searching the water for rodents.

"You know—get to know each other. Makes the trip less awkward. What are you looking for? Did you drop something?" the boatman asked, beaming.

"You told me to look out for venomous troll—"

"Oh, I was just playing with you!" the man confessed.

Heat crept up the back of Wally's neck and into his ears. No wonder Moriel still treated him like a child, as gullible as he was. Still, the man seemed affable enough, and he had a point. "Well, if getting to know each other is your aim, a name would be a good start. What shall I call you? 'Boatman' isn't going to do."

"Everyone calls me Q."

"Q?"

"It's a nickname. My full name is Quadarius Quirinus Quaglio the Third."

"Q it is, then," Wally said.

At dawn, Penelope's eyes blinked open. A strong desire to serve the master overcame the nearly equal desire to go back to sleep. Penelope stretched away her aches and rose, half frozen. She tossed a couple of logs on the fire and stirred up a flame before jostling Cully and Ander awake.

"C'mon, boys! Let's get to work."

"Aren't you going to cook some breakfast first?" Cully whined sluggishly. Penelope tossed a slab of jerky at him that ricocheted off his sleepy cheek. "Okay," he murmured. "It is going to be one of those days." Cully located the jerky and ripped at it with his teeth. He stumbled to his feet. "Come on, Ander. She may start throwing heavier things at us. Get some jerky and warm up by the fire."

With the growing flurry, Mack and his gang began to stir from their sleep. Gradually remembering their promise, they rose to help clear away the remnants of the destruction foisted on the Sanctuary by the Shadow. They separated the things that could be repaired from the things that were beyond repair, returning lightly abused objects to their proper places and sweeping up the rest. As they labored, a rustle in the foliage just beyond the perimeter brought all their efforts to a halt. Silently, they exchanged glances and dashed for their weapons.

When Master Chen emerged from the brush, pushing a wheelbarrow full of tools, he hardly seemed put off by the militants that faced him. "Well, good morning, my friends! Off to battle, are you?" They all lowered their weapons at once.

Penelope sighed as if she'd been holding her breath. "We thought you were asleep!" she said.

"Asleep? At this hour? Nonsense! As I said yesterday, we have work to do. Follow me." Chen rolled through the midst of the team, their eyes following him toward a path on the opposite side of the campus.

"Why do I get the feeling that he would be just fine here without us?" Mack said as he tossed the remains of a wooden bench on the fire and fell in line with the rest. "Where are we going, Chen?"

"Where very few have ever trodden, my dear Mr. Slade. And no, I would not be fine without you."

The party followed their ancient friend down a stone path so obscure and unassuming that no one would guess that it led anywhere important. The way was pleasant, shaded from the sun by a canopy of heavy green and lined with the last of the season's dainty, fragile wildflowers. The stone path ended at a carpet of moss, which led to an arthritic tree, covered in knobs and knots, at the edge of a precipitous ledge.

"You sure we're going the right way?" Mack asked skeptically. Chen ignored him but stepped forward and vanished.

"Master!" Peep screamed with a gasp.

Chen's wispy, white head reappeared from around the tree as if he were levitating above the ravine. "Well? Come on! No need to be afraid," he said and then disappeared again.

Penelope's pulse settled down and she inched forward, her arm extended behind her as if she hoped someone would grab her hand if needed. Then she sighed away her remaining fear. A mass of roots spiraled downward like a staircase. As a protection against the drop on the outer edge, a metal bar supporting a handrail had been installed. Penelope tested the stability of the protruding roots and, finding them quite firm, descended. The team followed. Surrounded by a densely forested expanse, the staircase emptied out onto a mossy green platform. Underneath the Sanctuary, a torchlit tunnel wended its way deep into the mountainside.

"This is where we leave our shoes, my friends," Chen instructed.

"But, Master," said Penelope, "must we?"

Just past the entrance, sharp, stony debris covered the tunnel floor. Chen said nothing. He just smiled placidly until the team began removing their shoes and considered the best way to maneuver over the jagged floor with the least discomfort. Chen strode into the cavern and passed over the rocky surface as if floating just above it.

Fenek took one look and turned around and headed back up to the Sanctuary.

"Fenek, where are you going?" Cully yelled after him.

"I ain't doin' it. I'm bigger than three of yous put together. That's gonna hurt!" he said and marched away.

Ander figured the best way to pass through the corridor was as quickly as possible. He was light and nimble and made it without too much difficulty. Penelope was more strategic in her method, placing her feet gently and slowly in the most accommodating spaces among the rocks. Then, Mack and Ike stumbled through erratically like baboons in a flood, wincing and grunting all the way.

Beyond the corridor, a blanket of cool, velvety soil soothed the team's tortured feet mercifully. And with the milky sheen that gleamed around and above them, the company soon forgot their pain and gazed in awe. The light pulsed slowly and gently like a shifting breeze in unison with a faint chorus of crystalline voices. It was eerily beautiful and strange.

Mack covered his ears and squeezed his eyes shut. His senses revolted. "What is that sound?" he asked.

"Tradition holds that it is the voices of the sages, serenading their king beyond the Wall."

"Sounds more like they're torturing him," Mack quipped, twisting a finger in each ear.

"I think it's beautiful," said Peep. She strolled through the cavern, studying the space as if trying to see through a frosted window. One path led around a corner and deeper into the mountain. Along the way, the opalescence glowed dreamlike, filling Penelope with intense peace.

Finding her way into a small room, Penelope noticed a dark hole, conspicuous for its contrast against the white glow. It was just large enough for a grown man to crawl through. She knelt down and peered in but could see nothing.

Ander came searching for her. "What did you find, Peep?"

"I don't know. There's another corridor here. But there isn't any stone inside. It's just dark."

"Maybe it's a storage space? Or they could have exhausted that area—mined all the stone out of it."

"I suppose," Peep said.

"Anyway, Chen would like us all to gather."

Penelope nodded, and the two returned to the main cavern.

"We are here for one purpose," Master Chen announced. "We must rebirth the Stone of Sages."

"But how?" said Penelope.

"First, we must maintain silence in honor and thanksgiving."

"I have to sit down," Mack said suddenly. "I don't feel so good."

"That is not too unusual, Mr. Slade. You may feel vulnerable or weak," Chen explained. "It is the exposure. Let the feeling pass through you. Don't resist it."

After a brief moment of silence, Mack stood. "Okay. Now what, Chen?"

The old man responded, "We must find a vein that will yield a large enough chunk of opal, extract it, and deliver it to the longhouse where I can shape it properly."

"Well, let's get to it, then," Mack said, lifting a pickax he had grabbed from above and thrusting it toward the cavern wall.

"No!" Chen replied frantically, grabbing the ax handle and deflecting it toward the floor. "We have ways of coaxing out the stone. We must first find the appropriate piece. Hacking away at a wall of sagestone is not only dangerous, it is profane. This is a sacred space. Our task requires time and patience."

"I have neither to give, Chen. This place is making me crazy. I gotta get out of here."

"Very well. We will have to do without you after all, Mr. Slade. We will manage."

Mack offered a quick nod of the head and then winced and grunted back through the corridor, with Ike and the Slade gang right behind.

"Well, Ander, Cully, my dear Penelope," said Chen, "It's up to us. Let's find that stone."

16
Death and Desire

"Why, no, now that you mention it, I haven't seen Haden in over a week," Josiah said as he scratched his chin. "You two are inseparable lately. I would think you'd be the first to know his whereabouts."

"That's the problem, Josiah. I don't," Moriel replied.

"Don't worry too much. He'll turn up. At his age, he isn't wandering too far from town."

"Not so sure about that," said Chaz. "He was ready to go hunt down Wally single-handedly when the kid failed to show in Dead Springs."

"If you think a search party is needed, you can count on me."

"Thank you, Josiah, I will let you know," Moriel replied. "In the meantime, I have some questions about your gemstone figurines."

"Oh! You want to buy one? I just got a bunch of new ones in yesterday. I can give you a good deal," Josiah offered hopefully.

"No. I have some concerns. These come from Josephine's mine, right?"

"Yes. She extracts them and has them cut."

"Has she ever tried to get you to push fire gems?"

"Josephine? You're talking about Josephine Pruitt?" Josiah's eyes bounced between Moriel and Chaz. Then, the merchant laughed in loud, undulating chortles. "You're crazy! Why on earth would Josephine do such a thing?"

Moriel and Chaz waited for Josiah to collect himself. This was no joke. When Josiah stopped laughing, Moriel said, "Josephine has fire gems among her collection at home."

Chaz elaborated, "You know that little girl that came into the store with her grandmother? They live in Smithtown."

"Yes, yes . . . Mrs. Dearing and little Hazel," Josiah recalled.

"Remember how she carried on about a red dragon she called Daniella? Josephine claims to have it and plans on giving it back to her. It's made of epithymite."

Josiah's levity dissipated. "Josephine would do no such thing!"

"She looked me right in the eye and told me the gem belonged to a little girl," Chaz replied.

"How do you know it was a fire gem?"

"I tried to pick it up. Stole every ounce of joy from my heart in an instant. That's how it ended up on the floor with a broken wing."

"Then she doesn't know what she has, gentlemen," Josiah emphatically declared. "I can't imagine she understands what she has."

Recalling their conversation at the Geyser, Moriel turned to Chaz. "Didn't you say that she handled the stone but seemed unaffected by it?"

"Yeah." The spark of thought lit in his eyes. "Do you think she is somehow immune to them?"

"No, but . . ." Moriel batted his lips with his forefinger before elaborating. "We know that epithymite affects people differently. Not all destructive emotions are as obvious as anxiety or sadness or rage. Ambition, for example."

"Longing," Chaz added.

"Vulnerability," Josiah Constance added sheepishly as he recalled his own battle with the mysterious mineral years earlier. "What if the gems amplify our individual weaknesses?"

"I am not one to pay much attention to women's fashion," Moriel said. "Does Josephine still wear that heart pendant that Asmodeus gave her? Wally once told Haden and me that she always seemed to behave like a smitten school girl when wearing it."

"Yes, now that you mention it, I do remember that about her," Josiah said.

"She was wearing it the day I dropped by her house . . . the house that used to belong to Asmodeus," Chaz said with foreboding. "As did her mines."

Josiah's stomach lurched. "Moriel! Whatever happened to Asmodeus?"

"No one knows. He vanished a couple of years ago."

"Perhaps one person knows," Mr. Constance suggested.

"Josephine," Chaz responded.

Moriel shook his head. "Impossible. We are just speculating here. On the surface, a case against her seems reasonable. Among other things, Asmodeus was a money-grasping, status-hungry aristocrat. He invested in mines. Josephine is a money-grasping, status-hungry widow. She now owns those mines. I can see why she would venture into his circle. But in the end, Josephine must have seen the villain for who he was—just as we did."

"Must she have?" Chaz cut in. "Or was she wearing his fire gem around her neck even then? Maybe even now? Ambition? Longing? How do we know she didn't help him escape?"

"On the other hand, how do we know Mrs. Pruitt is not in significant danger?" Josiah Constance added.

The door of the general store flew open, sending the string of jangling bells that hung from the handle in a bouncing, twirling ruckus. Sheriff Malvo from Smithtown rushed through.

"Sir Moriel! I found your friend, Haden. Crashed his rig by the West Wall Bridge on the way to Smithtown."

"Where is he? Is he injured?" Moriel asked.

"He's in pretty bad shape. Still breathing, but just that. He's over at the doc's. Doc doesn't think he can save him."

"Moriel, where's Waljan?" Mr. Constance asked. "He needs to be here."

But Moriel was out the door before Josiah finished his sentence.

Following Moriel, Chaz paused long enough to answer the lingering question. "No one knows where Wally is, nor has any means of communicating with him."

When Moriel arrived at the home of Dr. Fales, he didn't think to knock. He strode through the front door and proceeded to search every room for Haden Hunter.

Mrs. Fales approached him, worry creasing her forehead. "He's in here," she said, and led Moriel down a back corridor to an examination room. She waited at the door while Moriel rushed to his friend's side.

"You old troublemaker," Moriel said softly. "We've been worried about you."

Haden lay unconscious, taking shallow, rattling breaths. His face was gaunt, pale, and yellowing, his frame bony and frail. Cotton gauze covered his head like a winter cap.

"You need to hold on, friend. We're trying to find Wally. If you leave us now, you know he's going to take a pickax to Castle Wall just to reach you," Moriel chuckled through his tears. "And that's not going to go well with the king!" He dried his face hastily as Dr. Fales entered the room. "It doesn't look good, does it, Doctor?"

"I'm afraid not. He was crushed under his rig. Took a blow to the head, too. A lesser man would have been dead already. And at his age, with his health already compromised, he is one tough old man. Malvo had to put the mare down. She'd been tangled in a thicket with a broken leg."

"Thankfully he didn't have to witness that. He loved that horse," Moriel said. "Is there anything we can do to make sure he's comfortable?"

"It would be dangerous to move him any more than we already have, and getting him to take in medicine or food would likely choke him. Unless he wakes and tells us how he feels, we need to assume he's as comfortable as he can be."

Moriel nodded, his arms tightly folded over his chest.

"He was gripping this when the sheriff brought him in," the doctor said. Fales handed Moriel a piece of bark. "It's a message for Wally."

Moriel read the message:

My dear Waljan,
honor those you love, remain strong in the king.
I will wait by the castle gates.
~ Your dearest ~~friend~~ father, Haden

"Wally will be grateful. Thank you," Moriel said, and left the room. He found Chaz waiting in the entryway of the Fales home. "We have got to track down Wally."

"I can go out looking for him, Moriel, but honestly, I haven't the least idea where to start. He isn't in Mortinburg and he's certainly not at Eastern Ridge."

"I know where he could be. There's a spot by Castle Wall he visits when he needs to think. I will check that out. But he probably went back to Dead Springs to meet up with Peep and Culbert. Start there."

"But Moriel," Chaz said with resignation, "That will take days. I don't think Haden has hours."

"Neither do I. But that doesn't mean we shouldn't try."

The robust, mouth-watering scent of roasted scrub grouse filled the Sanctuary as Ander turned the spit one final time. His stomach grumbled loudly. Pulling the spit off the fire to cool, Ander set the rod across two stumps and ventured off to collect the others for a long-awaited meal. With an empty pot and a metal spoon he tromped through camp making a clatter. Fenek was the first to appear, followed by his brothers. Mack brushed by Ander and snatched the spoon out of his hands.

"It's a *sanctuary*, boy, not a base camp. Your voice is loud enough!" Mack scolded.

"Sorry. Just trying to get you guys fed!" Ander protested. "You want a personal invitation?"

Ike followed up behind his brother, saying, "Hey, Mack, the kid's getting cocky!"

Ander just smiled and continued in search of Penelope, Cully, and Master Chen. He found Penelope practicing with her bow while Cully repaired a chair leg. No one had seen Chen all day.

Penelope offered to track him down. "I think he's working in the longhouse. I'll go get him."

Ander returned to the firepit with Cully as Penelope packed up her quiver and headed off. She paused outside the door of the longhouse, hesitant to interrupt the meditations Chen performed several times a day. A hypnotic droning confirmed that the master was working. Master Chen often fell into a soft, mechanical humming when concentrating on a task. His low, lazy melody sounded more like a machine than a tune. Penelope knocked, and the droning stopped.

"Come in, child!" Chen called.

"How did you know it was me?" she asked as she crossed the threshold.

"I didn't," Chen chuckled. "No matter who you were, you'd be a child to me."

"Huh. I hadn't thought of that."

Chen's eyes remained fixed on his work. He sat at a make-shift workbench in the center of the longhouse, hunched over an enormous opal and drawing a rough block over its surface. In long strokes, the block created a soft grinding sound.

"Making progress?" Peep asked.

"Come closer," Chen replied as if suppressing a burst of unbridled joy. "It has been many years since I have practiced the art. But it looks like I haven't lost my touch!"

Penelope approached the workbench. On one side of the pearly lump, Chen had worn down a soft curve with a corundum whetstone. Pastel swirls shimmered across the creamy, smooth surface.

"It's beautiful, Master Chen!"

"Yes, it is. I just hope I can get this done before I need to replace these tools. I don't think I have any others handy."

"I saw some kind of storage cavern in the mine. I could go back and see what supplies are there."

"No, no. We don't have a storage space in the mine. Everything would be up here in the Sanctuary."

"What was that hole for, then? There was a dark hole along the floor, deeper in the mine."

"I don't know of any hole, my dear. But no matter. I'm pretty certain these will last. With effort and time, we will have a beautiful new stone."

"How long will it take?"

"It is hard to say. I must achieve the proper shape to amplify and stabilize its natural properties. Perhaps a few days. Perhaps weeks."

"Then you can teach me? You can teach me to use a speaking stone and talk to my parents?"

Master Chen set down his tools and rose from his workbench. "Penelope. I appreciate your desire. But a speaking stone serves alone those who walk with the king."

Penelope's shoulders drooped. "Yes. Of course." She turned to go, completely forgetting why she came in the first place. She turned back. "Why am I always denied the gifts of Abidan? You said that all the people of Mortania belong to the Realm. Have I not done enough for the kingdom?"

"My dear girl, you cannot buy your way into the kingdom either with gold or effort. Walking with the king is an invitation. All that is needed is that you respond."

"I don't know that I can do that. I mean . . . I can't understand what I can't see. I just don't have whatever it is that you and Wally and Moriel have." They stood silently a moment. Then Penelope asked, "You walk with the king. So maybe if I walk with you, that would be a start?"

Master Chen smiled. "Yes. I think it would."

"Oh! I nearly forgot. Our dinner is ready."

"What a relief! I could use some nourishment and rest. I have been breathing in the heavenly scent of roasted fowl for nearly an hour!" Chen replied.

Around the fire, the famished fellowship silently tore into their meal, serenaded by the pops and gasps of burning pine and cedar. With the warmth radiating around them and the satisfaction of food in their stomachs, it wouldn't be long before the gang were ready to end their long day in restful sleep.

Master Chenaniah broke the silence. "I am very grateful to you all for the hard work you have done. The Sanctuary is once again in suitable condition to house the Stone. And soon it will."

"Too bad that is all it will house," Mack suggested. "I hope you aren't planning to live here all alone, Chen."

"The Sanctuary exists for two crucial purposes: the protection of the mines of Shroud Peak and guardianship of the Stone of Sages. Agasti must always be present, even if alone. But even then, the Agasti is never really alone here. You see, the Stone of Sages brings the extended community of Abidan together in time and space, connecting all through the Realm. Without that connection, we lose our way. Community is essential to Abidanian life."

"Yeah, well . . . you know what I mean. Alone on *this* side of the Wall," said Mack.

Penelope looked up from her meal, perplexed. "Master Chen, you said my parents were in the Realm. How can that be? They were not Abidanian."

"They are now," he said with a warm smile. "We don't understand all the ways of the king, Penelope. Being an Abidanian doesn't mean we have achieved some level of accomplishment or understanding. It merely means that we desire and seek the friendship of the king and respond to his friendship to the extent we are able."

"But why would they seek the friendship of someone they don't even know?"

"How can one seek friendship otherwise? Doesn't the seeking suggest the object is unknown? You are friends with young Mr. Slade here, are you not?" Chen asked. Ander blushed.

"Of course," Peep replied.

"But you don't know him as thoroughly as you know Waljan of the Realm, who has been your friend since childhood. You are closer to Waljan than to Ander. Yet you still recognize Ander as your friend. I imagine that your parents died before they knew the king well. But they knew of him enough to seek his friendship. And that is what counts most—the *desire*.

"Many people believe that those who've reached the Realm are somehow different from the rest of us—born of nobler stock, let's say. But we are all destined to live as sages in the Realm, not just the knights or the Agasti or those who die in defense of the king. All of us. What defines a sage is not his ability or wisdom, his power or experience, but his relationships. An Abidanian is one who loves the king and his people. And it takes no time at all to choose love."

"This is all so confusing!" Mack exclaimed. "If I had known years ago that one day I would be helping to restore the mother of all death stones for a crazy old man talking about lovable kings and hidden realms, I think I would have questioned my sanity. I mean, who could have imagined it?"

"Death stones, Mr. Slade?" Master Chen replied.

"Where we come from," Ander explained, "sagestone, or something very much like it, is known as a weapon. The fear of it is spread through stories, but also through experience. We call it white gall."

"I have never heard of such a thing," said Master Chen. "The very idea is repulsive to me."

A growing concern overtook Penelope. "Master Chen. Back in Dead Springs you also told me that shattered sagestone was . . . what did you call it . . . volatile. Dangerous. What did you mean?"

"Well, I certainly didn't mean it should be used as a weapon!" Chen huffed, explaining, "If fractured in just the right manner, and combined with certain elements, sagestone will amplify and release its stored energy along the cleavage planes in the form of intense, explosive heat. Thankfully, sagestone is one of the hardest minerals in Mortania. It is not easily shattered."

"Certain elements . . . ," Penelope mused. "You mean for example . . . epithymite?"

Thoughtfully, Master Chen nodded, "Yes, in theory. But to my knowledge that has never been tested. One doesn't come across sagestone shards easily."

Fenek looked up from the meal he'd been devouring. "I dunno 'bout that. The rope guy in Housh sure had a bunch of 'em. He tried to sell me some." Even in the dim firelight, Fenek could see his friends' faces pale. "What?"

"Maybe it *has* been tested, Chen," said Mack. "And that explosion was Housh after all."

"Maybe that's why sagestone has a reputation among Slade's people," Cully offered.

Penelope anxiously added, "And maybe that's what this attack on the Sanctuary was all about. Cully, how sure are you that we collected every last shard of that stone?"

"How could I possibly know that? I had no idea how large the stone was or what its shape was. I know I got everything I could. What are you thinking?"

"Master Chenaniah," Peep said, "if the Shadow Assassin had taken some of the shards, what kind of destruction could they unleash?"

"That depends," Chen replied. "Even a small amount could be dangerous. If we had recovered none of the shards, I wouldn't want to contemplate the potential."

"Hold on . . ." Peep's voice quavered, "Master, you said that you were not familiar with the hole I found in the mine. What if someone was here when we were in Dead Springs? What if someone extracted some opal from the mine?"

"That would be a very dangerous and foolish endeavor," Chen replied.

"But would that deter someone like the Shadow?" Peep asked.

"Likely not," Chen answered.

17
Something Coming

Worry and dread accompanied Wally down the underground waterway. Quadarius kept the barge at a steady pace, poling from bow to stern and back. Periodically, the quant would tap against the rim of the boat, sending hollow drumlike tones echoing throughout the gray underground. With the creaks and groans of wood and metal, the *kerplunk* of falling droplets, and the sloshing current, the tones tripped out a percussive lullaby.

Wally gazed into the darkness, spotting nothing but the dancing reflections against jagged lines of protruding rock. Sleep beckoned. But Moriel's chastisement, Haden's disappointment, and Sir Eban's cold pragmatism ceaselessly cycled through Waljan's brain, denying him rest. A quiet sea ditty broke through the chatter in his mind.

> *And the seagulls are calling, "Away, push away!*
> *The sun is escaping the day, push away."*
> *Liquid gold sky drains below the horizon*
> *And ushers forth heavens of gray, ev'ning gray.*
> *Away with the tide, push away.*

"I haven't heard that one," Waljan interjected.

"Haven't you?" Q asked. "My father used to sing it to me

when I was a child. He was a navigator on a large merchant vessel. Loved to sing. Nice strong voice, too."

"Well, I'd say he passed it on," Waljan said with a warm smile.

Q returned to his songs and Waljan to his worries and nothing more was said for miles. With each passing hour, Waljan's apprehensions and fears intensified. Finally, a dim light eased into the cavern from a distance and appeared to snake toward the barge. With it came a heavy rushing sound.

"We're coming to Whispering Gorge, sir," said Q. "I'll let her drift awhile with the current to allow our eyes to adjust to the sunlight."

"Great. We must be close to Housh, then," Waljan said.

"Yeah, it's just south of us."

"Let's head over there."

"But, Sir Waljan, I heard Sir Eban specifically direct us north toward Mortinburg. It's going to delay us."

"I am aware of that, Q. But I need a few supplies. I had no time to prepare for a trip like this."

"But, sir, you know as well as I that Housh has been destroyed."

"I know that there was an incident at Housh. Neither of us knows to what extent."

"Well, all right, then," Q replied.

The sun had passed its height and pulled the day along with it. Hidden beneath a dark bed of clouds, it denied Waljan and Q any relief from the chill of the cave. The barge emerged from the cave mouth and into a downpour that relentlessly pocked the river's choppy surface. The men had just enough time to secure a deer hide tarp over the barge. It wouldn't keep them dry for long.

"It looks like heading to Housh is the best option, after all," said Waljan. "We can wait this storm out a bit and get warm."

Within minutes, the barge cleared a rocky cape, revealing the dismal bank where Housh once stood. Not much remained but ash and charred debris. Q poled the boat up to shore among the charred remnants of a dock bobbing in the shallows. Neither men had suitable words to utter. Like synchronized robots, they jumped out of the barge and moored it to a small boulder by the shore. Then, they sought shelter from the rain under an indent in the cliff wall.

Silently the men began collecting pieces of the abundant charcoal and bits of wood. While Q retrieved a net from the barge to throw for fish, Waljan started the fire. Bo Dog scampered off to take inventory of the complex scents that hovered about the destruction, returning only after the fish had been caught, cleaned, and cooked.

"We're traveling upstream on our next leg. I think it best we stay here until morning." Q suggested.

"You're the captain," Waljan replied, watching the skies as the rain gently subsided. "Q, you wouldn't happen to have a nautical scope in the barge, would you?" Waljan asked.

"Now, what kind of a captain would I be without a glass? Why do you ask?"

"I just need to take a look around. Gather some information before we lose the light."

Since landing, Waljan could not think of anything but Peep and Cully. He and Bo Dog wandered along the bank, trying to spot the suspension bridge to Miqodesh. Walking south along the waterline, Waljan scanned the opposite wall of the gorge with the telescope until he spotted the dangling planks and rope that no longer traversed the expanse.

I must find out if they arrived at the Sanctuary! Waljan thought. Maybe he could convince Q to take him to the other side. It would only add two days to their trip. Surely they could afford two days.

Waljan and Bo Dog made their way back to their camp through what used to be the center of the market. The cheerful bonfire greeted them, but the boatman was gone. Waljan yelled for Q and sat down to warm himself. No one replied. He beckoned the boatman again. Nothing.

"Come on, Bo. Let's go find out where Q went." Bo Dog just

whined, preferring to dry his coat by the fire. "Fine. Stay." Waljan grabbed the glass, headed down to the bank, and spotted Q milling about the barge. The clouds parted in the distance, allowing the late afternoon sun to break through.

"Hey, Q!" Waljan called. The boatman looked up and frantically began pushing the craft into the water. "What is he doing?" Waljan thought aloud, and with growing concern, dropped the scope and sprinted toward the bank. "Stop! What are you doing?" Quadarius continued to push the boat and, finally getting it far enough out, climbed aboard and located his quant pole.

By the time the boatman had plunged his pole into the water, Waljan had reached the shore and dove for the boat. "Q!" Waljan screamed again. "Wait!" He swam to the boat, climbed up the side, and flipped his legs over the edge.

"Leave me alone! I have to get to the sea!" Quadarius urged.

"What are you talking about? What's gotten into you?" Waljan pulled the quant out of Q's hands and knocked him away, poling the boat back to the shore.

"I must go! There is no time to lose!" Q pleaded, jumping on Waljan's back and knocking the pole into the water. Q pulled him backward and wrestled him to the floor as the pole sunk to the bottom of the river. The boat began to drift.

"Q, let's talk about this! I can help you!"

"You just want to stop me. I have to go!" Quadarius responded.

Waljan freed himself and tried to toss the mooring line toward land. But Q tackled him, sending both of them and the line overboard. Q tried to drag Waljan underwater. Swimming out of reach, Waljan made it to the shore with the line in hand. He glanced back at the boatmen, who followed close behind. Waljan dropped the line and tumbled up the bank to gain his bearings. Quadarius rushed toward him. With a well-timed swing, Waljan clocked Q hard in the jaw. As Q hit the ground, something flew from around his neck and nestled among a pile of rocks.

Waljan ran back to the bank only to watch the barge slip out of sight, headed downstream.

"We've lost the barge! What is going on, Q?" Waljan barked as Quadarius rose slowly to his feet, panting and rubbing the side of his face.

"I don't know! I had this overwhelming need to get to the sea—to find my father!"

"Your *father*? Now? This is something you have to do now—all of a sudden?"

"I . . . I . . . ," said Quadarius, blinking.

"Where is he?" Waljan asked.

Q rubbed his eyes and looked around him. "I . . . don't know. No one knows. He was lost at sea when I was a boy."

"Do you get this strange urge often, or just when you are on an important mission? How are we going to get off this shore?"

"I am sorry, Sir Waljan. This has never happened to me before. We can flag down another vessel. The boating community is a helpful bunch." Quadarius scratched his head. "I really don't know what came over me."

Waljan studied the boatman's distraught expression and sighed in resignation. Q was clearly as confused about his behavior as Waljan was. "I think you lost something when you fell, by the way."

"Oh?"

"Yes. I heard it land over here," Waljan said, taking a moment to search the rocks.

"Oh, yes. Must be that bobble I found among the debris. Some kind of jewelry."

A glint caught Waljan's eye. He stopped. A heart-shaped gemstone sparkled crimson in the sunshine. "Q. That isn't a bobble."

The hum of fellowship mingled with hushed expressions of concern and hope as the Abidanian community filed out of the caverns at Eastern Ridge Falls. This was their sacred gathering site where they met regularly to perform the Mist Rite, a ritual of communion with the Realm. This particular night the Abidanians appealed to the king on behalf of their dear friend Haden Hunter, who remained in the care of Dr. Fales.

The mist chamber was nearly empty when Tyre Pruitt offered to replace the torches in the hall. With his arms full of freshly pitched batons, he made his way out of the chamber toward the mouth of the cavern, placing each dying torch in a bucket of sand against the wall. Then, he set a fresh baton in the bracket and continued down the hall.

When he reached the last bracket, Tyre turned around and lit the row of new torches as he made his way back to the mist chamber. Moriel waited for him there.

"There is someone here to see you, Tyre," Moriel said. "I'll be outside."

In the back of the mist chamber a woman awkwardly stood. "You're wanted in three municipalities. The people of Smithtown are furious. I figured you'd be hiding out here."

"Mother. How did you . . ."

"Oh, this cavern is not new to me. I haven't been here in many years, but once it was almost like home." She sat down by the pool to quell the shaking in her legs. "It is difficult to return."

"You are returning to the community?" Tyre asked with a hopeful lilt.

"Don't be ridiculous, Tyre. Of course not," Josephine quipped. "But I did think I at least owed you some kind of parting word. A goodbye."

"Goodbye? Where are you going?"

"Well, that's not important. You are looking well. Mr. Myrtle told me you were very ill. It seems Moriel's remedies have been effective."

"I think it's just good genes, actually," Tyre replied with a sad chuckle. He hoped the comment would elicit some congeniality between them. But Josephine stared at her shoes.

"I don't understand why you have done this," she said at last.

"Mother . . ."

"Please, Tyre. Let me finish. You are a grown man now. I can understand you wanting to establish your own way—to set yourself apart. A mother half expects her children to push her away at some point. But *this* way? Betraying your brother's memory? Your father's memory? Aligning yourself with the enemy—those who took the life of your very own family! It is utterly shameful."

"Mother, I had nothing to do with what happened at Smithtown."

"I know. I am not referring to Smithtown. You and I will likely not see each other again. But I wanted you to know that I have not abandoned you. *You* have abandoned *me*. And while I still love you, I doubt I can ever forgive you for that. I also want to say that I am sorry for whatever pushed you to this, and for what is coming." Josephine stood abruptly and walked briskly out of the chamber.

"Mother? What's coming? Mother!" But Josephine did not stop, and Tyre thought it foolish to run after her. Without a word, Josephine passed Moriel at the mouth of the cavern. He returned to the cavern to check on Tyre.

"You okay?" Moriel asked.

"She apologized for something that is 'coming,'" said Tyre. "I have no idea what she means."

Moriel furrowed his brow. "Did she say anything else?"

"Only that she'll never forgive me."

"Oh. Well, that's not very reassuring, is it?" Moriel replied.

"I don't recognize my mother any longer. Something has changed. Drastically. The depth of her gravity is uncharacteristic. I mean, I don't mean this to be insulting to her, she always took good care of my brother and me. She doted on us. But she's always been so concerned about superficial things. I thought people like that were unaffected by tragedy. Now she is serious and sullen. I miss her smile."

"Superficiality is often a defense against tragedy. But it only goes so far. Your mother has sacrificed more than she believes is fair. Many would feel the same way in her place. I understand how difficult this is for you. But it's not really about you. Your mother is angry at Abidan. She needs our understanding. Let's go home. It's been a long day."

Just above the cavern, Josephine Pruitt met up with a tall, elegant gentleman who had been waiting for her with the horses. Night had fallen, and the stars eased into place, one by one.

"Well, are you satisfied?" he asked.

She glared at him without a word and mounted a beautiful black stallion. It tossed its glossy mane and pounded the ground, waiting impatiently for permission to run. The horse spun around with excitement. Finally, she said with determination, "We start here."

Her companion settled into his saddle. "My, Josephine, you do have a flair for the dramatic!"

"It's not drama, my dear. It's justice." She slapped her horse hard with her crop and took off into a full gallop through the wilderness. Her companion followed with a throaty laugh.

18
Help from Beyond

For a day and a half Waljan and Quadarius remained stranded, trying to flag down the few transports and crafts that made their way up the river. No one seemed eager to risk picking up two stragglers. They would have considered walking back to Mortinburg through the Crescent mountain range had they known about the primitive trail that brought Master Chen and the gang down to Housh.

"I thought you said the boating community was eager to help one another," Waljan complained.

"Maybe the setting is making them suspicious. We just have to keep trying," said Quadarius.

"Maybe we are just asking the wrong people for help." The light of an idea flickered across Waljan's face. "Of course! I don't know why I didn't think of it earlier! My speaking stone may be dead, but we can take our needs straight to the Realm!"

"Here? In the middle of this destruction? We would need a mist pool," said Q.

"I am a Knight of the Realm. I carry the waters of Eastern Ridge everywhere I go. All I need is some kind of bowl."

Looking around, Q found an intact oyster shell. "Will this do?"

"I guess we'll find out," Waljan said and he entered into the Mist Rite.

Arising from the sacred waters, a mist enveloped the men. Silently they offered pleas of assistance to the sages of the Realm. The mist dissipated, and they returned with renewed hope to the banks of the river.

Many more craft traveled south in the opposite direction of Mortinburg and often slowed to ask about the plight of Housh. They all seemed too shocked to offer aid and shuttled quickly away. But a pleasant break came the third day.

As Waljan and Q set fish traps for breakfast, the bow of a familiar craft came into view downriver.

"Hey, Q—that looks a lot like your barge, doesn't it?" Waljan suggested.   "Mine is a pretty standard design, Sir Waljan. I don't think I could identify my own boat from this distance."

"Yeah, but it is coming this way, and your boat or not, I am going to be on it. Where did that nautical glass go?" Waljan searched around and spotting the scope, picked it up. He trained the glass on the approaching barge. "For the love of all things good, I don't believe it!"

"What! Is it ours, Waljan?" Q asked in suspense.

"Ours and more, my good boatman! Woo-hoo!" Waljan tossed the glass over to Quadarius and whistled for Bo Dog. The dog lumbered over to his master's side, bounding through the water as Waljan waded out, waving his arms like a madman. When Bo Dog finally recognized the pilot of the barge he began to bark gleefully. "Culbert Longbow! Cully! It's me! Wally!"

"You know that man?" asked Q.

"Know him? He's practically my brother! And that is definitely your barge. The barge must have drifted to the opposite bank!" Q stood, dumbfounded. "Okay—I know how unlikely it seems. But he has been staying at Miqodesh. He probably came down for supplies and found the boat."

Cully navigated over to the bank, where Q and Wally caught the line and secured the boat to the shore. Like a freshly caught salmon, Bo Dog flipped and waggled and twirled in excitement, impatiently waiting for his friend to hop out of the boat. As soon as Cully landed one foot in the river mud, Bo Dog leapt up with wet dog kisses.

"Down, Bo! I'm coming, I'm coming. Good boy!" After a quick pat, Cully headed straight for Waljan with a bear hug. "What on earth are you doing here, Wally?"

"It's too long a story, so I'll ask you the same thing."

"Hey, Wally!" A deeper, slower voice came from the barge. Fenek clumsily rolled out of the barge and plopped onto the beach with a thud. Then, both men took in the destruction with awe. "Whoa," Fenek said.

Cully shook his head. "We saw the smoke but were hoping it wasn't this."

"Pretty bad, huh?" Waljan remarked.

"Yeah. The big guy and I are on our way to Mortinburg to find Moriel and speak with the council. We have been in the Sanctuary. Chen is trying to restore the Stone of Sages."

"He can do that?" Waljan asked, wide-eyed.

"Apparently. We extracted a hunk of sagestone from the mine beneath the Sanctuary, and he's been working on it for days."

"And how long will it take?"

"No one knows. Chen doesn't even know. It's been decades since the Sanctuary has produced a new stone. But he's definitely making progress."

"But will it be soon enough? We still don't know what the Shadow is planning, if anything. I'm also on my way home to speak to the council. Eban is starting to understand how Maweth is getting away with these attacks."

"We have some ideas of our own. Perhaps together we can sort this all out."

"Oh! I nearly forgot. Culbert Longbow, this is my friend, Quadro . . . Quen . . . uh, Q the Third. Q, this is my good friend, Culbert Longbow." The men shook hands.

"Quadarius Quirinus Quaglio the Third, to be exact. But, everyone calls me Q for obvious reasons."

"It is very nice to meet you, Mr. Quaglio," Culbert said with a smile.

"Show-off," Waljan quipped.

"Thank you, Mr. Longbow, for returning my barge."

"*Your* barge?" Culbert asked.

"Yes," Waljan replied. "Part of the long story I mentioned. It got away from us and drifted downstream about three days ago. I was hoping for royal intervention."

"Well, the sages are working overtime on this one. We were hoping to avoid trudging along the banks for days on end. Your beautiful barge was waiting for us at the base of the mountain trail as if it were arranged! All we had to do was find a good-sized branch to push us along."

With two extra passengers, the barge made steady progress north through Whispering Gorge. Not only could the men propel the boat double-time from both sides, they could do it through the night by taking shifts. Even against the current made heavier by the rain, Waljan still managed to make up at least one day lost.

Thoroughly exhausted, dirty, and bedraggled, the men finally arrived at the river port in South Mortinburg. They booked a couple of rooms in a boarding house on the edge of town while poor Bo Dog spent the night alone in the barge. After a warm bath, a hearty meal, and a solid night's sleep, they were as good as new.

In the morning while Cully and Fenek still slept, Waljan joined Quadarius on the docks to see him off and retrieve Bo Dog. "Thank you for your service, Q. I do appreciate it despite our mishap."

"Once again, I am very sorry for my behavior, Sir Waljan. I hope the delay doesn't cause you any trouble."

"It wasn't your fault. I'm glad you got your barge back. Give my regards to Sir Eban." Q pushed off, singing a little sea ditty as he slipped away.

Waljan and Bo Dog headed toward Caddock General Goods. A few townspeople who hadn't seen Waljan now for at least a month greeted him warmly. But he soon realized that something was not right. Several passersby stared at Waljan grimly or with grave concern in their eyes. Acquaintances clearly avoided him, and many he expected to see were absent from their normal routines.

Waljan arrived at Caddock's and pushed through the swinging door. "Hey, Josiah!" he said, approaching the counter.

"Wally! Where have you been? Everyone has been searching for you!" Josiah cried out in relief.

"They have? What's going on?"

Josiah opened his mouth and then shut it again. "Uh. Oh well, I think you better go see Moriel. It's really not my place to . . . I mean. Moriel is over at the Geyser."

"At this hour? The Geyser is usually closed until after lunch."

"Yes, well. There is a gathering there. They would want you to be there. You know, the Twelve and many of the community."

"Well, that explains why you're one of the few familiar faces I've encountered all morning. This is perfect. I have important news from Dead Springs," Waljan said.

"Okay, then. And Wally . . ." Josiah stared intently into Waljan's eyes, "If you need *anything*—anything at all—just ask. I am here for you."

"Uh . . . oh . . . kay, thank you, Josiah. That is very kind. Nice to see you."

With a nod Waljan left the store and, shaking his head, walked over to the Geyser. The tavern was packed and bustling. As he entered, the throng hushed and parted, making a clear path to where Moriel stood speaking with Sir Allred at the bar. Shivers immediately shot up Waljan's spine. It felt as if he had walked in on something he was not prepared for. He took a few tentative steps, flanked on either side by his Abidanian community, and spotted Tyre.

Waljan thrust his hand out and, grabbing Tyre's, pulled his friend into a warm hug. "Tyre, buddy, you look great! Are you all healed up?"

"Yeah, Wally. Good as new." His words were warm and

appreciative, but his eyes were sad.

"Good. Okay. Hey . . . what's going on?" Waljan noticed the long table of refreshments. "Having a bit of a party, huh?" he asked, despite realizing that the atmosphere in the room didn't fit a happy occasion.

"Of sorts. I think you should go talk to Moriel."

"Yes. I have news. From Sir Eban." Waljan patted Tyre on the shoulder and tried to compensate for the growing discomfort in his gut by addressing the entire crowd as he approached Moriel and Sir Allred. "I have unfortunate news from Sir Eban of Dead Springs. I have just arrived by barge through Whispering Gorge. The Shadow continues his attacks, the latest one against the merchant port of Housh. I am sorry to say it was completely incinerated."

The room broke into gasps and whispers as Waljan continued. "There is nothing left but ash and debris. The Shadow . . . ," he hesitated as he caught Moriel's eye, "or whoever wants us to believe in it, left his calling card."

Waljan held up a packet of wrapped-up leaves bound with a ragged twine of roots. He placed the packet on the bar and unwrapped it, careful not to come in contact with the surface of the heart-shaped fire gem that Quadarius had found.

"But I also have good news," Waljan continued, now certain he had everyone's rapt attention. "Sir Eban thinks he's discovered how the Shadow has pulled off his attacks. He believes we can now develop a strategy for stopping him." Waljan delivered Eban's letter to Allred. "It's all in here."

"Well done, Waljan," Sir Allred said. "We will need to convene a meeting of the Twelve as soon as possible. But not today, urgent as it may be. Tomorrow afternoon; and we will notify the community as soon as we have decided how to proceed. Moriel, I would like you to attend the council, and if you think it possible under the circumstances, Waljan should accompany you."

"Of course, Sir Allred," Moriel replied.

"Circumstances?" Waljan asked.

"We have bad news as well, Wally," Moriel admitted.

Waljan glanced around to find that everyone remained still, all eyes locked on him. He tried to ignore it. He was more concerned with finding Haden among them. But the old man was not there.

"Moriel. I need to see you and Haden privately . . . it's . . ." Moriel stopped him. "Wally . . ."

"Please, Moriel, I'd like to finish." His voice began to crack. As long as he could avoid hearing the news he now expected, he could suspend the truth that much longer. "I need to apologize to *both* of you."

Moriel hugged Waljan firmly as if preventing him from crumbling into a thousand pieces. Then he placed his hands on Waljan's shoulders and tried to break the news with a single look.

"Moriel? Where's Haden?" Waljan studied the crowd, a sea of sympathetic eyes. His stomach lurched and his voice grew frantic. "Haden? Haden!"

"I am sorry Waljan. We tried to find you in time," Moriel explained.

"No! He's not gone. He's not gone. Tell me where he is!"

Moriel hung his head. "We just placed the stone this morning."

Waljan bolted from the tavern.

"Waljan!" Moriel pleaded and started after him. But Sir Allred held him back.

"He will need some time, Moriel."

Slowly the memorial resumed, and the conversation turned from happy memories about Haden Hunter, trapper and part-time store clerk, to concern for Waljan's well-being having lost his dear friend in such an abrupt and ill-timed manner.

Several hours passed before Moriel approached Waljan and Bo Dog at the graveside. Bo Dog lay in the center of the freshly mounded dirt. Off to the side, as if discarded, Waljan's spirit sword stuck deeply in the ground at an odd angle. Moriel yanked it out and presented it to Waljan, who sat behind the grave with his back against the headstone.

"It seems you dropped this," he said. Waljan didn't make eye contact but grabbed the blade carelessly and dropped it at his side. Moriel sat next to Waljan and stared at the clouds passing by overhead. "He knew. He knew you were sorry. He knew you would come around. And this is the last thing he wanted."

"Everyone knew he was ailing but . . . what happened? Or do I not want to know?" Waljan asked.

"It was a freak accident, Wally. Bella ran the rig off the road. By the ravine on the way to Smithtown. No one passing by noticed it until it was too late."

"Stupid old codger, riding alone," Waljan grumbled.

"Well, you know Haden."

"*Knew* Haden," Waljan corrected.

"Know. Know Haden. Haden Hunter, Sage of the Realm and all the more ready to help when we need him."

"Yeah, sure. I'll just sing him into being with my trusty speaking stone. The stone that's now a useless hunk of rock."

"Wow. Of all people, you would be one of the last I would expect that kind of cynicism from. Did you expect him to live this side of the Wall forever, Wally?"

"It wasn't supposed to happen like this, Moriel. Not like this," Waljan lamented. "I should have been there for him. I should have been able to say goodbye."

"I have a funny feeling that he is not too worried about it now. Imagine what he is experiencing this very moment."

"I don't have to. I've been there. At least . . . I thought I had been there. I am not so sure anymore. Nothing is happening the way I expected. Sometimes I wonder if this is all a sophisticated fantasy—playacting. Like children do. I have my sword and my costume. My celebrity. It's all just pretend." Wally rubbed his sore eyes. "How's Bella?"

"We had to put her down," Moriel replied. "Haden never knew." Wally nodded his appreciation for that. "I have something for you. Something Haden wanted me to give you." Moriel handed Waljan the bark on which Haden had scratched his goodbye. Waljan barely got through it before succumbing to a renewed flood of tears. The two sat in silence, missing their friend together until the last rays of sunlight slipped away.

19

Goats or Lambs

Broken and drained, Waljan expended all his remaining energy sitting through the council proceedings held the afternoon after his return. He surprised himself in caring about the fate of Mortania. His grief was so raw. But he did care, even still. He despised the evil that Maweth unleashed on the world as much as he missed Haden. And he knew that Haden would want him to do everything he could to bring that evil to an end. He imagined that Haden was on a mission of his own. And, after all, he was. Haden had traveled to Castle Mount, beyond the Wall, and was enjoying the privileges of court as all Abidanians hoped to one day.

The council read the letter from Dead Springs in the company of those gathered. It recounted how Sir Eban combined the shards from Miqodesh with the fire gem Mack Slade left behind. They produced controlled explosions, infernos, and energy discharges. Based on the amount of material used, he calculated that a weapon could be devised to trigger scheduled destruction. Such a weapon might create the illusion that an evil power was able to commit great harm, undetected.

"I believe," Sir Eban concluded in his letter, "that we must act quickly to stop these attacks and bring the culprit to justice. It seems to me that they are increasing in frequency and intensity."

Despite the letter, the council remained unconvinced. The motive was as mysterious as the perpetrator. And there were practical issues as well.

"My friends," Sir Allred argued, "the possibility that our perpetrator used sagestone and epithymite to achieve a controlled attack against Mortanian villages seems plausible. But where would he have acquired sagestone, let alone the epithymite?"

Cully knew he could provide a partial answer. "Excuse me, sirs."

"And who is this young man?" Sir Allred asked.

"Culbert Longbow, sir," Cully replied. "My companion Fenek Slade and I have been sent here by Master Chenaniah to deliver a message to the elders. We were among a group that has been staying with the master at Miqodesh and grappling with the same question. You're aware that the Sanctuary was attacked in a similar way to Smithtown, Housh, and other communities. As you also know, the Stone of Sages was completely destroyed. We tried to recover all of it, but the master is concerned that some of it may have been taken during the attack."

"But you are talking about a very small amount of sagestone in that case," Sir Allred said. "How could that make much difference?" One of the elders leaned in to Sir Allred and spoke quietly to him. Allred nodded and addressed the room, "Sir Filbert brings up a good question. Do we have any evidence that sagestone and epithymite were both present at any of the incidents in question?"

"No, sir," Moriel responded.

"Actually, we do," Cully interrupted. "The day before the attack, a vendor in Housh tried to unload fractured sagestone on Fenek Slade, one of my traveling companions. Fenek's here in Mortinburg. You can talk to him if you wish. Days later, a boatman from Dead Springs found that heart-shaped fire gem—the one Wally delivered to you yesterday—in the rubble in Housh."

"That's not definitive, Mr. Longbow. You can't be sure the fire gem was there at the time of the explosion. It could have been dropped afterward. But it is suspicious at least. How can we know where this evil will strike next?" Sir Allred asked.

"We don't have to know," Cully suggested. "If each town knows how these attacks are carried out, they will at least know what to look out for in preventing another."

"But it will take weeks to inform every community in Mortania. Especially without speaking stones," Waljan said.

"We can't help individual towns," offered Moriel. "If we stop the attack at its source, we may be able to save Mortania itself."

"What do you mean, Sir Moriel?" Allred asked.

Moriel looked over to Waljan. "Thanks to the diligence and wisdom of Sir Waljan, we know that the perpetrator—the Shadow—is likely based near Mount Sar. It makes sense. Sar contains the largest deposits of epithymite. I think we need to call the knights together and plan a mission to Mount Sar."

"But, Moriel," Allred countered, "if we cannot easily warn each town without employing the network of speaking stones, how are we going to rally the knights together in time?"

"Leave that to me," Moriel answered.

If their trust in Moriel was insufficient, the lack of a better option forced them to agree. The council adjourned, slightly encouraged. Waljan and Cully followed Moriel out of the building.

"Moriel," said Cully, "how are you going to get the knights together?"

"I have no idea, Cully. I am willing to entertain yours."

"Don't look at me!" Cully replied with his hands up in surrender.

"Moriel!" someone yelled from down the street. It was Tyre Pruitt. He was flushed and out of breath.

"You look horrible. Has that fever returned?"

"No. Worse," Tyre said.

"Come with me. We can talk over at Josiah's. Fenek and Chaz are waiting for us there."

Josiah prepared an early dinner for the men as they settled

into the dining room to discuss plans and hear Tyre's story. Though the news was not a surprise, it confirmed fears they hoped were overblown. Confused by his mother's strange visit at the cavern, Tyre had decided to return the gesture and pay her a visit at the house. He hoped that if he explained his reasons for joining the Abidanians, she would understand. But as he reached the grand gates at the end of her drive, he noticed a handsome carriage parked in front of the house.

A tall man in top hat and tails stepped out. Tyre dodged behind a low-growing hedge and observed the visitor between clumps of teardrop leaves. The man checked his surroundings carefully and then proceeded into the house. Tyre slipped through the gate and rushed toward the house, skirting along the shrubbery for cover.

The windows on the side of the house that faced him were obscured by a large walnut tree and a yard full of overgrown flora. He sidled up to the brick facade and peered around the corner. Presently, two figures left the house.

"Well?" said Josiah Constance. "Who were they, lad?"

"Mom and Asmodeus Capra," Tyre said with heavy concern. "They got into the carriage and headed north."

"Asmodeus?" Waljan spewed like soured milk.

Tyre nodded.

"What is he doing here?" Chaz Myrtle asked. "I was hoping none of us would see that fiend again."

Tyre paced the floor. "Why is she still hanging around him, Moriel? I don't understand."

Moriel's heart ached for the boy. Josephine was not the only one who had been stripped of family. She failed to see how her son suffered all the worse for her rejection. To turn on her son while in close association with Asmodeus seemed to Tyre a much more profound betrayal than his association with Abidan. Josephine might say it came down to a difference in perspective.

"I don't see that we can avoid the truth any longer, gentlemen. What we have been calling the Shadow is none other than

Asmodeus Capra, and Josephine Pruitt is implicated with him," Moriel said regretfully.

"Not my mother," Tyre said quietly. "She wouldn't do these things."

"No. Not under normal conditions, Tyre. But there are a lot of extenuating circumstances. And the evidence points to her. We know that epithymite can be weaponized. We know that Josephine has been distributing it and that she holds the deeds to Asmodeus's mines. We know that he has returned and that he is capable of great evil. And we know your mother is still associating with him. The only remaining mystery is why."

"He's tricked her," said Tyre. "Like he once tricked me. It's that gem she wears. I know what that's like—I have felt the power of fire gems. Wally, you understand. Either one of us could be in her position. We have to save her, Moriel!" Tyre urged.

Josiah Constance entered the room with a trayful of drinks and warm bread and sat down among the men. "Tyre is right. Josephine is not responsible as long as she wears that necklace."

"She is not entirely guilty. But she is not entirely innocent, either," said Moriel as gently as possible. "We all want to help Josephine, Tyre. At this point, we don't know enough to take any definitive action. We need to find out what Asmodeus is planning."

"How are we going to do that?" Chaz asked.

"We could follow them," Josiah suggested.

"But we don't even know where they're going or whether they'll return," said Chaz.

"No, but I just happen to know where they'll be in two days. Little Hazel Dearing is expecting a personal visit from Josephine. I heard her grandmother mention it yesterday when she was in the store."

"Well, that's a start," Moriel interjected. "Chaz, do you think you can watch the grandmother's house and then follow Josephine and Asmodeus, unnoticed?"

"Sure, there's plenty of time to get there," Chaz replied.

"Okay. If Josephine returns home, meet us back at my cabin in forty-eight hours. But if she leads you down to Mount Sar, find out exactly where she ends up. Then return to the Sanctuary. Wait there for further instructions."

"I've never been to the Sanctuary. I'll need a guide," Chaz said.

"Fenek and I can tag along," Cully volunteered. "I'd like to check in with Peep anyway."

"And what shall I do?" Josiah asked.

Moriel sat back in his chair. "You have already done so much, Josiah. You're not even Abidanian and yet you are always ready to help when we need you."

"I don't need to be Abidanian to be your friend. Nor am I spared the threat that Asmodeus poses. And I certainly don't want to see anything happen to Josephine or any of you."

"Come to think of it, you have a lot of people coming in and out of the store, and a lot of them are from out of town. You can help me spread the word among the knights who come through Mortinburg."

"Absolutely," Josiah said.

"Okay, then," said Moriel. "Tyre, we'll do everything we can for Josephine. But you have to be strong. Things may not play out as you wish. Do you understand?"

Nodding, Tyre looked around the room. He tried to compose himself but, failing, stood up and left the room. Waljan followed.

Moriel sighed and rubbed his forehead. "Let's move on. If Chaz fails to find a base on Mount Sar, Wally can take us to where he was ambushed by the Slade brothers, and we can start there." He turned to Fenek. "Are you and your brothers still interested in hunting down the Shadow?"

"Nothin' would make Mack happier then stickin' it to Maweth," Fenek replied.

"That's a story I'd like to hear some day," said Moriel.

"He don't like to talk about it. Neither do I."

"Are your brothers still at the Sanctuary?"

Fenek nodded. "They was supposed to stay put 'til we got back."

"Good. We'll stage our next move there," Moriel decided.

Waljan caught up with Tyre, and they walked silently through town for some time. Words were unnecessary. Waljan's presence spoke plainly. Finally, Tyre stopped and watched the sun descend as if it interested him.

"You don't have to be here, Wally," Tyre said.

"Sure I do," Wally replied. "I'm your friend. And I know how alone you feel right now. No one should ever feel that alone."

"How did you do it? When you first arrived in the city, how did you handle the abuse that Caddock and I dished out, not to mention Mom's demands and Asmodeus's scheming, all while missing home? Where did you get the strength?"

"I never had any strength. I had to lean on my family."

"But you didn't have a family."

"I had Haden. And I had Abidan. They were my family. They *are* my family. They're yours, too."

"Come on, Wall . . . I mean a *real* family. Real people, not some sage from a storybook."

"Tyre, during the Mist Rite, what do you see in the mist?"

"Water vapor."

"Come on, Tyre. I'm serious. You've never seen the beautiful colors, the sweeping landscapes, the king in white with gold trim?"

"No, Wally. I want to see it. I trust that it's there, but all I see is mist."

"You trust that what's there? A storybook? Imaginary characters?"

"You know what I meant," said Tyre.

"I'm not sure *you* know what you meant. Everyone wrestles with doubt, and often times we say things to convince ourselves that we really believe in what we are told is true. But I have seen what awaits us—at least if my eyes and imagination were not conspiring against me. Those beyond the Wall aren't bogged down in fear and heartache and judgment. They are totally free. And they want us to be free, too. We can count on them to help if we ask."

"That doesn't help Mom much, does it?"

"My mom lived under a boardwalk for ten years, Tyre. If there was hope for her, there is hope for your mom, too."

20

The Bargain

The nip in the air signaled winter's approach. While Asmodeus's carriage hurried through the countryside, Josephine watched the leaves snap gently off the passing trees and flutter to the ground. She studied the manner in which the winds reshaped clouds every few minutes and made the grasses in the fields undulate like the sea. After a while, she stopped seeing what lay beyond the carriage window and focused instead on the memories that crowded her mind.

"A penny for your thoughts and not a cent more," Asmodeus said.

"Just taking in the view, my dear."

"Oh, how utterly boring," he replied.

"You bore too easily, Judge."

"It takes no breeding nor accomplishment to enjoy the simple things in life. I much prefer contemplating the wealth and power I will accumulate when our plans are complete. When we bring all of Mortania to its knees, we'll show the people who truly deserves their allegiance and loyalty: Asmodeus the Just!"

"And . . . ?" Josephine prompted.

"And what?" he replied.

"And . . . what about me?"

"Oh, of course. Asmodeus the Just and his queen, Josephine," he answered with a hint of dismissiveness.

"Don't worry, dear. You don't need to make me any promises. I will be content in teaching those Abidanians a lesson for what they've done. What happens after that means very little to me."

"You can't possibly be serious, Josephine. Why settle for revenge when I can give you the world as well?"

"You can't give me back my sons. Nor my husband, for that matter."

"Are you still pining away over them? Really, Josephine. You have *me*. Many would say you have made out for the better in that exchange."

"Hm." Josephine smiled pleasantly at Asmodeus, but her eyes remained listless and empty.

"Honestly, I was never all that impressed with you," Asmodeus elaborated. "But this thirst for revenge you've fostered is a start, at least. You are redeemable."

"That's rather ironic," Josephine said with an edge. "When we first met I had no inclination for revenge and I thought you were the most interesting man I had ever met. I guess people change."

"Oooh . . . biting. Very clever, my love. You've made out for the better, after all!" Asmodeus said smugly. "How gratifying."

Josephine quickly changed the subject. "I do want to inspect the mining operation this week, if you don't mind."

"It was already on the agenda," Asmodeus replied.

The rig slowed and came to a stop. "We're in Bluewater, ma'am," the driver announced.

"Oh, very good." With a syrupy air Josephine added, "I trust you will stay here, my dear?"

Asmodeus unleashed his habitual sarcasm on Mrs. Pruitt. "No. I think I will visit the fish monger and have a chat about whether he prefers fileting to deveining. Of course I am going to stay here! Quickly now, or I will leave without you."

"You wouldn't dare. I know too much for you to cross me now," Josephine replied, and marched off to her destination.

Asmodeus just laughed at Josephine's audacity. She had once been a frivolous, superficial gossip. But in Asmodeus's company and in his estimation, she had evolved into a graver, darker, festering soul. He began to see her less as a tool and more as an ally. A short while passed before Josephine returned to the carriage.

"So who is the lucky recipient this time?" Asmodeus asked.

"A shipping magnate. The owner of Shoreline Marine Company. Big donor to the Abidanians in Bluewater. He wanted a set of rubies for his leading executives. You could say I delivered more than he bargained for."

"Oh, you are a very clever girl, Josephine. I wonder, though, are we not going a bit overboard? At this rate, all of Mortania will be up in flame, including you and me!"

"Are you nervous, Asmodeus? I must say I have never detected cowardice in you before."

"*Me?* Don't be ridiculous. Nothing you do could possibly frighten me. Just remember, my dear Mrs. Pruitt, if we are to rule this world, there must be some of it left when you are done."

"I am very aware of that," Josephine replied.

"So where is our first delivery tomorrow?"

"Smithtown. A little girl is waiting to be reunited with her Daniella."

The following day, Asmodeus's carriage arrived early in Smithtown, rolling past the tavern where Malvo and Fenek waited. They left their drinks and followed the carriage down the street. A block away, Chaz and Cully watched the carriage pull up in front of the Dearing house. Josephine got out of the rig, walked up the porch stairs, and knocked on the door. As she entered the home, greeted warmly by Mrs. Dearing, Bruce Malvo and Fenek approached the rig and rapped abruptly on the side.

Asmodeus opened the carriage door. "Yes? What do you want?"

"Sheriff. Please step out of the carriage, sir."

Asmodeus exited the rig, loaded with a ready set of insults

and affronts. "We have just arrived in town, sir. What could you possibly want from . . . Malvo!" He dropped his speech and let out a hearty laugh. "Why, you dog, I thought you were dead!"

"No, boss. Still howling at the moon. How are you?" Malvo chummily asked.

"Couldn't be better! You're sheriff, I see. Still at it, keeping the riffraff in line."

"No better way of beating the law than being the law. Isn't that what you always say?" Malvo quipped. Asmodeus tipped his topper in reply. Malvo continued, "I've heard you've been lurking around but didn't expect to see you here."

"You heard? From whom?" Asmodeus inquired. "I haven't been making a point of it."

"Well, I have a few tricks up my sleeve. I've learned quite a bit since we last saw each other."

"I'm not sure I like the sound of that, Malvo."

"Ha! Nothing a powerful guy like you needs to fear. In fact, that's what I wanted to talk to you about. I saw you roll into town and I just had to introduce you to my friend, Fenek Slade. He's a bounty hunter from overseas. A tough nut. But I have no work for him here. None that can take advantage of his full potential, if you know what I mean."

"Perhaps," Asmodeus said, holding out his hand to Fenek. "Very good to meet you, Mr. Slade. You are a strapping young man, aren't you? And what a grip!" Asmodeus pulled his hand out of Fenek's and massaged it gingerly.

"I was hoping you might be able to use him in one of your operations," Malvo explained. "He really needs a job."

"Have you ever worked in the mines, sir?" Asmodeus asked.

"Uh . . . You mean digging? I can dig. I dug a few graves in my time."

Asmodeus raised his eyebrows. "Aha." He turned to Malvo. "I'm sure I could find him something. I'm headed to the mines today in fact, as soon as my companion is finished with her visit.

Do you have a horse, Mr. Slade? The carriage is a bit small for someone of your substantial frame."

"Ya, I gots a horse. An' two friends. Can they come, too?" Fenek asked, trying to appear dimmer than he already was.

"Sure, why not! The more the merrier. Have them saddle up and wait for the rig to pull out. We're headed south."

"Okay. So we'll follow yas. But if it's all the same to ya, we'll hang back a bit. I'm kinda 'lergic to dust," said Fenek.

"Fine, fine. Go saddle up," Asmodeus said, dismissing him with a flutter of his hand before offering it to Malvo. "Good day, *Sheriff*. So glad to know there is an ally in Smithtown should I need one."

"Here to serve, boss," Malvo said with a wink. He returned to the jailhouse, offering a thumbs-up as he passed Cully and Chaz. Within the hour they were on their way with Fenek to the Shadow Assassin's base, willingly lead by Asmodeus himself.

Sparks flew with a clang of blades. Leaning in, captivated, Tyre nearly slid off the fence rung where he sat. Moriel wielded Paraclete with effortless grace, while Wally's Bergdis met his opponent with youthful fury and strength. Paraclete ricocheted off Bergdis over and over as the two knights clashed, swinging, blocking, lunging, and deflecting.

Between breaths, Moriel stopped to explain the moves and modifications Tyre could make for his much smaller dirk. They had no plans to enter battle, but Moriel always preferred to travel the wilderness with trained fighters when possible. A few pointers would help a little.

As the morning slipped away, the men began packing and prepping for a long trip south. At Waljan's suggestion, they opted for a paddle craft over horses, as the river would take them straight through Whispering Gorge and to the base of Miqodesh. There, they would meet up with the Slades and the Longbows. All that was left was dinner, relaxation, and waiting on Chaz to return. If he didn't show up, they would head out the next day.

While enjoying Moriel's warm stew, Wally looked about the room where, years ago, his mentor nursed him back to health. This had been home for a few glorious months of recuperation, training, and learning. His eyes fell on the mantelpiece, where Moriel had always kept the largest intact speaking stone Wally had ever seen. Next to it sat another stone he recognized, the one he found in Mrs. Pruitt's guest room just after moving to Mortinburg. He'd forgotten that Moriel had taken it away at her request. And then, he remembered something else.

"Moriel, do you know a man named Bart?"

"Who?"

"Bart. I met a man named Bart the day after we found Tyre in Smithtown. He wanted me to give you this." Waljan handed Moriel the leather pouch that he had kept since his encounter in the wilderness. Moriel's face turned ashy and his hands began to shake.

Offhandedly, Tyre said, "My dad's name was Bart. Well, Bartholomew. But Mom called him Bart."

As if Tyre wasn't even there, Moriel asked, "Wally, I don't understand. Where did you say you got this?"

"I got it from a man I met in the woods between Smithtown and Mortinburg. He said you would know what it meant." Watching Moriel unravel emotionally was like watching a mountain crumble. "Are you okay, Moriel? What? What is it?"

Moriel examined the pouch, inside and out, running his fingers over the embroidery. "BP," he said, alarmed. "Um . . ." He took a breath. "I don't know who it was you met in the forest." Moriel showed Tyre the embroidery. "But this belongs to Bartholomew Pruitt."

The young men sat, speechless. Moriel stood up and approached the mantel. He took the stone that he had removed from Josephine Pruitt's home and tucked it snugly into the pouch. It fit perfectly.

With great significance, Moriel wrapped the leather cord around the pouch, returned to the table, and thoughtfully handed the bundle to Tyre. "This is yours now, son." Tyre took the pouch and touched it solemnly as if his father still clung to it somehow.

"Bartholomew was—*is*—one of my dearest friends. I wouldn't be here if it were not for him. I wouldn't be who I am. He taught me all I needed to know about the king and his ways. But as you boys know, he has been gone for over twenty years." Moriel pulled himself together, wiping his face with a kitchen rag. "I don't know who you met, Wally, or how he got this pouch. And I don't know what game he's playing."

Tyre was more hopeful. "Wally, you have the gift of seeing. Could it have been . . . ?"

"Nah, Tyre . . . come on," Waljan protested. "All that seeing stuff is just really overblown."

"Wally, just tell me what he looked like? Did he look like me?"

"No," Waljan said as he tried to reconstruct Bart's face in his mind. Deflated, Tyre slumped back in his chair. As realization bloomed on Waljan's face he continued, "But he did look like Caddock."

"Tyre, weren't you two twins?" Moriel asked.

Tyre nodded his head. "But fraternal. I look more like Mom. But Caddock . . ."

Moriel pushed his chair back and stood. "We all need to get some sleep. We'll leave first thing in the morning." Moriel muttered his good-night as he headed for the loft, grabbing a bottle from the kitchen shelf. His footsteps fell heavy on the ladder, and he disappeared into the dark.

First thing in the morning turned out to be noon. Waljan and Tyre were packed and waiting for Moriel hours before he finally descended the ladder, groaning and groggy. He milled about, refused breakfast, lingered at the bathing bowl, and couldn't decide whether he had overpacked or forgotten something critical to add. Even after they did hit the road, their progress was painfully slow for Tyre and Wally. It was midafternoon by the time the three men had loaded a wherry at the dock and shoved off. But now, at least, they could rely on the currents that would deliver them to Miqodesh in just a few days' time.

Over the first day and into the second, Moriel's energy and wits returned. But the peace that usually characterized him was gone. Quiet hung in the air like an arrow reaching maximum height, on the verge of falling back to earth.

The three travelers took watch in shifts. Tyre had just finished his watch and quickly fell asleep in the bottom of the hull. Wally had just woken up, and Moriel sat at the rudder, somber and focused.

"Moriel," Waljan asked cautiously, "you're worried, aren't you?"

Moriel noted the concern in Waljan's eyes. "Not in the way you think I am."

"What way is that?" Waljan asked.

"Wally. I am not a mind reader. You have not been fully weighed and measured. You're not laid out before me like an open book. But I *do* know that you fear I think otherwise. We are both discovering what you are capable of. And I have great expectations and hopes. But that doesn't mean that you are not bound to a nature that binds all of us. What I know about you is that you are a young man. And young men have tendencies.

"You are not me. But you are enough like me that my age and experience can predict with some accuracy how you might behave in some circumstances. It's not a slight against you, your skills, or your personality. It's simply an awareness of our nature. And that's how I know what you think. It's also what I'm worrying about. I'm not worried about an assault on Mount Sar. I'm not worried about Josephine or Asmodeus. I'm worried about what truths they will twist and how it will affect you."

"Why would anything Asmodeus say affect me? I know he's a liar."

"Best not to underestimate your enemy. Just *trust* me."

21

New Alliances

"If these guys keep showing up, Mack, I'm not going to have enough stew to feed them all!" Ander complained, stoking the fire. "Where are all the men coming from?"

"I don't know, kid, but it's a good problem to have. Don't worry. We'll take a hunting party out and bring in something bigger to add to the pot," said Mack.

"We may not have to," Ike Slade added, as a new stream of men came into the Sanctuary, carrying pounds of fish from the river, a bundle of quail, and a young buck.

Knights of the Realm had started to arrive the previous day, first one at a time, then in groups of three or more. Now, several dozen men crowded the Sanctuary, all asking for Moriel of the Realm. But the Slade brothers hadn't seen Moriel for weeks. They had no choice but to pull Chen away from the stone to manage the situation. Wearily, Master Chenaniah left the longhouse, supported by Penelope, who took his arm and escorted him to the open courtyard where the men gathered.

"My dear brothers," Chen announced with as much volume as his weak voice could muster. "What can I do for you?"

"The question is, what can *we* do for *you*?" one knight replied. "We have all received a general request through Mortinburg to meet with Moriel of the Realm here at the

Sanctuary of Miqodesh. The call was urgent and of great importance to all of Mortania. But that's all we know."

"Your devotion is great, and the king will undoubtedly reward you for it. I will tell you what we know. You have all by now heard the rumors about Maweth, the Shadow Assassin, and the mysterious arson attacks that many towns in the region have suffered. It would seem that we are close to finding this villain and need your help in tracking him down. I expect that Moriel will arrive within a matter of days with more information. For now, that is all I know. Rest, eat, and welcome to the Sanctuary." Chen turned to Penelope with an expression she understood, and the two immediately headed for Chen's hut.

"You have had a long day at the stone, Master," Peep said. "Let's get you situated, and then I'll bring you some dinner. Ander has been working on preparing a delicious stew."

"Thank you, my child," Chen mumbled.

When Chen was settled and comfortable, Penelope returned to the courtyard for food. Dodging the swarms of mingling men who greeted friends, dumped packs, cleaned weapons, and milled about, she heard her name faintly from the Sanctuary trail. *Wally?* she thought.

"Peep!" she heard again.

"Wally? Wally!" Penelope hustled toward the voice, gently pushing her way through the crowd. As she avoided the last human obstacle, Wally caught sight of her and the two collided in a warm embrace. Waljan lifted her clear off her feet.

"You're safe! By the mercy of the king!" Waljan said. "Where's Ander? Is he well?"

"Right as rain," Penelope replied. "He's over at the pit making his everything-goes-in-it stew. And Tyre? Is he better?"

"Right as rain!" Waljan replied with a smile. "We came in together. He's with the Slades." Then Waljan's cheer evaporated like summer rain. "Haden's gone. He climbed the Wall, Peep."

"Oh no!" Peep said, giving Wally a sincere and consoling hug as tears filled her eyes. "But, that's . . . good, isn't it? I'm so sorry, Wally."

"Good for him, yes. I have to keep telling myself that," Waljan said.

"You must miss him horribly," she added.

Waljan brightened a little. "I want to show you something. Look. He wrote this for me." Waljan handed Penelope the piece of bark that Haden used to write his last words: *Your father, Haden.*

Penelope took Waljan's hand. "He was a good father, Wally. You will have that memory always." She smiled and wiped her nose and cheeks. "Hey, did Cully meet up with you?"

"Yeah—he went with Chaz and Fenek to scope out Mount Sar. They haven't returned yet. But have I got a story for you! You won't believe it. . . ."

Penelope interrupted. "Oh, I'd like to visit with you, Wally, but I can't right now. The master is waiting."

"Oh? He's still sick?"

"No, he's fine! Well, tired. He's been working on restoring the stone. It's just that he's expecting dinner."

"Oh . . . okay. I guess I'll catch you later?"

"We'll see. If he can spare me," Peep said, leaving Waljan standing there awkwardly. Waljan would not stand for long. There was too much to do.

With Moriel now in the Sanctuary, briefing the recruits and making plans would take a good portion of the evening, but not before a solid meal. A few of the men lent Ander a hand, and additional meats were added to his stew. Others foraged roots and greens for the pot, and many just ate from their own stores of dried fruits, biscuits, and jerky. When everyone had their fill, Moriel laid out the potential need to go into battle.

"What kind of army has the Shadow gathered?" one man asked.

"We don't know," Moriel replied.

"And his weapons? What should we expect?" asked another.

"At this time, we don't know."

A third asked, "Where will the battle take place?"

"Most likely on Mount Sar, but we don't yet know for certain."

Finally, a gruff block of a man asked, "Well, for love of good glory, what do we know for certain?"

"We know for certain that we must put an end to the terror that has gripped our communities and that we await news from our scouts. My friends, I have not called you here lightly. I appreciate your time, and I ask your continued patience for the sakes of our families and friends."

"Sir Moriel," came a voice from among the men. A knight of about thirty years of age stepped forward. "My name is Tillit. You have been a great friend of the king, and I will wait for your orders." Many among the crowd followed with expressions of general agreement, and the conference came to a close.

In the wilderness of Mount Sar, Chaz, Culbert, and Fenek trotted wearily behind the carriage carrying Asmodeus Capra and Josephine Pruitt. It stopped in front of a reinforced tunnel cut into the side of a steep incline. Stepping out of the carriage, Asmodeus motioned the riders forward. Fenek dismounted and approached, as Josephine tumbled out of the carriage with her cumbersome skirts gathered up in her arms.

"We leave the horses," Asmodeus said.

"Oh. Okay," Fenek replied in his dull fashion. "I'll tell the guys." Fenek led his horse back to Chaz and Cully and engaged in a short dialogue as Asmodeus waited with increasing impatience.

"Well? Are you coming or not? I have important work to attend to!" Asmodeus yelled to the three. Fenek handed his reins to Cully and lumbered back to the tunnel, tweaking Asmodeus's short temper.

"Okay. So, the guys are kinda scared of dark places. I have to do a little convincing 'em. Can we meet you? I mean, we don't want to keep you, but this may take a while. I think they have closet-tropia and . . ."

"Enough! It's *claustrophobia*, you half-wit, and they should have known that joining a mining crew might be a bit problematic for people afraid of confined spaces. Fine. Go. When you are done babysitting, continue down this tunnel. Do not veer off the main arterial. Doing so would most certainly end your life. There is a maze of tunnels within, many that have been out of use for years. If you lose your way, it is unlikely anyone will find you. The main tunnel will emerge on the other side of this ridge at the mining site. When you get there, ask for the Mayor. Tell him you are here for work. Got it?"

"Yep. Thank you, sir."

"Remember. Stay on the well-traveled path," Asmodeus emphasized.

"Main path. Got it." Fenek snickered softly as he rejoined his friends. Together they watched Asmodeus and Mrs. Pruitt disappear into the tunnel. The carriage swung around and took a southern road, leaving the three happily alone to make their next move—reaching the ridge above.

A small clearing off the road led to a patch of creek-side grass where the men could feed and water the horses. They tied the horses to a stand of trees and began a grueling ascent through dense terrain, over jagged boulders and up steep inclines until they emerged at the rocky ridge overlooking a vast mining operation. A dusty bowl of ochre and gray, the land had been stripped down to its rocky base, devoid of any vegetation. Like ants, hundreds of people labored, backs bent to their tasks, amid groans and shouted commands. They moved in and out of tunnels cut into the mountainside. Containers of glittering red mineral lined the perimeter.

"Peep was right! They are mining fire gems!" Cully exclaimed, wide-eyed. "We have to get back to the Sanctuary."

"Not yet," Chaz advised. "I want to see what kind of security we are up against."

"I don't see none to speak of," Fenek noted. "Some guys is shoutin' orders, but they gots no weapons."

"Maybe they don't need weapons," Cully wondered. "Maybe Asmodeus is using the fire gems to enforce his will."

"I don't think that would be enough," said Chaz. "Epithymite may weaken the will, but it can't take it over completely. Asmodeus must have a crew of intimidating thugs at least."

Just then, a fight broke out among a group of workers. Four muscle-bound hulks ran over to the scuffle and pulled the workers off one another.

"See?" Chaz said. "Asmodeus does have guards. They're taking those people away." Chaz observed a little longer. "I don't think they will be a match for a band of Abidanian knights."

"Let's hope Moriel has been able to scrape up a few," Cully said. "We need to shut this operation down."

"I can help!" shouted a man from behind them. Fenek had a blade out and ready to strike within less than a second. The grubby man shot his hands in the air. He was thin and ragged, and his gaunt face was hidden behind a thick brown beard. His haunted eyes pleaded for mercy. "Please. I am Odie Cluny. I escaped the mine and have been hiding out here, hoping to find a way to free the miners. I have friends down there."

"If y'escaped, then ya know who owns this mine, and who recruits report to," Fenek suggested.

"This is Core Mining Company, owned by Asmodeus Capra, and his site manager is called the Mayor.

Fenek nodded to Chaz and Cully.

Chaz introduced them. "We represent the Knights of Abidan." Odie just stared, blankly. "We're stationed on Shroud Peak at the Sanctuary of Miqodesh," Chaz explained. "Have you heard of it?"

Odie shook his head. "No."

"Well, we can take you back there, get you food and medicine if needed, and you can advise us on how to proceed."

"I can't leave," Odie said. "There is someone I left behind, and until I know her fate I am determined to stay here. I am safe. The mountain protects me. I'm relaxed, the mountain supports me. I am well. The mountain provides."

"Um . . . okay, good to hear, but are you sure you don't want some kind of help?" Chaz prodded.

Odie just shook his head saying, "I lost my desire." The men were not sure how to respond.

Chaz just moved on. "Well, let's make a fire and have some food. And you can tell us everything you know. How does that sound?"

Odie sat down on a stump and stared at the ground, waiting for whatever came next. The men concluded that whatever he had been through warranted as much compassion from them as they could afford.

By morning, the relief of food, warmth, rest, and companionship seemed to have restored Odie's senses. The men convinced him to accompany them to Miqodesh with the promise that they would reunite Odie Cluny with his friends from Core Mining Company.

Three days later, Moriel and the Slade brothers received the scouts' report in private and decided to take immediate action.

"It looks like a straightforward mission," Cully explained. "I think Asmodeus was counting on secrecy and fear. Pretty weak weapons against steel and courage."

"It seems too easy, though." Moriel worried. "Mack, what do you think?"

"I agree. It's too easy. But I don't know that it makes any difference with the significant amount of sagestone we suspect he has."

"What significant amount of sagestone?" Chaz asked.

"There's an entire mountain's worth under the Sanctuary," Mack replied. "Chen took us there to find a chunk to replace the Stone of Sages. Penelope discovered a newly dug chamber where mineral had been extracted. But it wasn't dug by the Agasti. Master Chen confirmed it. Our best guess is that someone came into the

Sanctuary after Chen was taken into Dead Springs to recuperate."

"Then Peep was doubly right!" Cully said.

"I hope not," Moriel countered with foreboding. "I shudder to think that sagestone has fallen into the wrong hands. But even if Asmodeus doesn't have plans to weaponize it, any operation producing the amount of epithymite that you saw at Mount Sar means trouble. Asmodeus is mining it for some kind of criminal purpose. We don't want to find out the hard way what that purpose is."

That night, the knights would make final plans for a rescue on Mount Sar. In the morning, they would follow Moriel and his company south. But first, they enjoyed a great feast, breaking bread as a family and drinking to the king. Those from North Bay to Dead Springs, from Mortinburg down the coast to Hidden Cove all put their differences aside in the service of their fellows. Laughter and the telling of great deeds culminated in song.

Together we march and together we fall
Together we rise on the side of the Wall
Where the wine is eternally flowing for all
So we drink to the will of the king!

No matter what comes, you, my brother, remain
And my sister through him, when again he will reign
Over all of his people, united again.
So we drink to the will of the king!

The rousing melody inspired Waljan to seek out Peep. But neither she nor Master Chen were present for the feast. Wally walked the grounds, searched the longhouse, asked around, but no one had seen them for hours. Quietly, he approached Chen's hut and tapped gently on the door.

"Excuse me, Master," he said in a near whisper. "I am looking for Penelope."

"Shhhhhh!" harshly emitted from inside. Penelope popped

out silently and closed the door as gently as if it might otherwise break to pieces. Then she sighed. "Why are you bothering him?" she scolded.

"Uh . . . I'm not trying to . . ."

"Is this important, Wally? I told you I wouldn't have much time. The master is very fragile and has been working night and day on that stone. I am very worried about him."

"Oh. I understand, Penelope. It's just that I expected you to have some dinner. . . ."

"Thank you, but I ate with Master Chenaniah," Penelope said. "And I'm beat. I think I will get some sleep."

"Good idea. We'll be heading out early tomorrow to take Mount Sar."

"Be safe. When you get back, I will have more time," Peep said.

"But . . . you're not coming?" Wally asked in disbelief.

"Wally! I've told you . . ."

"Yeah, yeah . . . the master needs you," Waljan replied. "We *all* need you, Peep. You are the best shot I know. You know we need an archer like you along. You can't stay here and play nursemaid. Ander can do that!"

"First of all, I am *not* playing nursemaid. Secondly, I will let Ander decide for himself what he can and can't do, and thirdly, you of all people should know that we need to replace that stone, and Master Chen cannot do it alone."

"So this is an ego thing?" Wally challenged.

Penelope looked as if something in her had shattered. "Apparently it is for you. Good night, Sir Waljan," she said soberly and walked away.

22

Revelations

The November rains let loose on the company as they trudged through Cloakwood. The Slade brothers took the lead. Having hunted both man and beast in these woods gave them a navigational advantage. They reached the mouth of the tunnel on Mount Sar but remained under cover, just beyond the forest edge along the road. Two of the men scrambled up the ridge to peer over. The mine was completely abandoned. Not a soul stirred below.

"It must be the weather," Mack suggested.

"Maybe," Moriel replied. "Fenek, are you sure Asmodeus didn't suspect you?"

"He's a sly one. But I don't think he caught on," said Fenek.

"Okay. We're going in. I'll take Wally, Sir Tillit, and the Slades. That way we can separate in pairs if necessary. Chaz, you stay behind with the rest. Keep out of sight. We'll run lines and tug twice if we need you. Once we have scouted out the tunnels, we'll go to phase two."

At his request, someone handed Moriel three coils of rope. He fastened one end around his waist and handed the extra ropes to Tillit and Ike to do the same. Then they crossed over the threshold.

The shaft was far wider than it appeared from the entrance. When their eyes adjusted to darkness, they could make out the faint bluish light that traveled through from the other end. They walked cautiously and quietly, trying to pick up on any sound that might give away a living presence. But nothing seemed to move.

Passing the entrance to an arterial tunnel, Moriel peered in. Fenek tapped his shoulder and indicated potential danger with a shake of his head. But Moriel knew that he wouldn't find what he was looking for at the opposite end of the straightaway. He needed to know what else lay within the mountain. He nodded his understanding and unsheathed Paraclete. Moriel signaled for the team to break up—Wally with Ike, Tillit with Fenek, and Mack with him—each taking a different passage.

Above, the ropes steadily traveled across the ground like ragged snakes into the mine. As the men descended farther into the labyrinth, someone yelled for more slack. They had to quickly tie off additional lines to lengthen each as the men continued their descent. An hour passed.

Circling down a spiraled shaft, Moriel led Mack into a widening antechamber. Ambient light was emitted through a portal ahead. Moriel crept forward. Against the wall, he leaned into the next room and beheld an enormous, sagestone structure. Jagged edges jutted out in all directions like an exploding star and vibrated ominously. A disturbing hum seemed to penetrate and cloud Moriel's mind.

Erected on a platform in the center of the room, the structure was surrounded by evenly spaced epithymite stones. The fire gems randomly set off sparks and bolts of red light that arced to the opalescent sagestone. In front, one gem seemed to be missing.

Moriel whispered back to Mack, "All clear, but we have some seriously dangerous minerals in here. Come look at this!"

Mack entered the room, and his heart skipped. "Whoa!"

Presently, Tillit and Fenek appeared from the back of the chamber just moments before Waljan and Ike emerged at Moriel's left.

"Well, gentlemen," Moriel said, "It looks like we have

stumbled on a highly explosive situation, if you'll excuse the pun."

"I'm guessing this could bring the entire mine down," said Mack.

"How do we know that it wouldn't bring the whole mountain down?" Waljan asked. "We have no idea what this thing can do."

"We should *not* be in here," Fenek suggested.

"Yeah, well—we are, and I am not going to leave without dismantling this . . . whatever it is. Everyone, back away." Moriel slowly edged toward the apparatus, flinching with each discharge of energy.

Waljan scolded him. "Moriel, what do you think you're doing?" But Moriel just waved him back.

Close enough now to touch the nearest fire gem, Moriel slowly extended his hand. The stone percolated with sparks, and Moriel withdrew his hand reflexively. He decided to try knocking the gems off the platform with his sword. As he extended Paraclete toward the epithymite, the sword quivered. Inches from reaching the first fire gem, the point of the blade lurched. *ZAP!* A bolt shot up the sword and into Moriel's hand. With a howl of shock and pain, Moriel threw Paraclete across the room and flew backward, his hand blackened and smoking.

Waljan ran to Moriel. "Are you okay?"

Moriel groaned and rolled on the ground clutching his hand. "I will be," he grunted. "It's just a hand."

"It's just your sword hand," Waljan said, helping Moriel to his feet. "We need to get you out of here."

"No, Wally. I'll be fine."

"So now what?" Mack said.

"I'm not sure, but I have an idea," Moriel replied, still wincing in pain and leaning against the cave wall. "Wally, do you remember how Sir Eban neutralized the Stone of Sages?" Moriel asked.

"Yeah . . . the mist pool."

"We have an army's worth of stable sagestone topside," Moriel continued.

Waljan caught on immediately. "Yes! That's brilliant!"

"Tug your lines, boys. Let's get everyone down here. When they arrive, they'll need their speaking stones." Moriel retrieved Paraclete and awkwardly sheathed it with his good hand.

"I don't get it, Moriel," Fenek mused as he stared at the opalescent beauty of the structure that continually threw random threads of energy around the platform. "Why would Asmodeus want to detonate his own epithymite mine? That doesn't even make sense."

"Oh, come now, really?" said a silken, baritone voice from the right. Asmodeus, followed by Josephine Pruitt, came forward through a fourth passageway leading into the chamber. "Even a brainless bullfrog like you can see the practical use of such a threat. Pending doom can be very motivating."

"So you are here, after all," said Moriel.

"What kind of host would I be not to greet my guests, hmm?" Asmodeus said with saccharin cordiality.

"We were hoping a dead one," Waljan snapped.

Asmodeus locked onto him with a sinister chuckle. "Why, it's Waljan Woodland! Still as impulsive as ever, but with a much darker sense of humor. I like that." He sauntered toward the center of the room, with an exaggerated sense of purpose and importance, Josephine always a step behind. "How is that moldy hunter you used to hang around? Oh . . . oh yes, he's *dead*. That's right." Josephine stopped in her tracks as he continued, "I thought I recognized Haden's smell as we passed the wreckage on our way to Smithtown."

Rage welled up in Waljan like a cresting wave as he reached for his sword. Moriel stayed his hand.

Undaunted, Asmodeus rambled on. "He was still alive then but struggling. My word! That man had a remarkable will to live. Isn't that so, Josephine?"

Mrs. Pruitt seemed confused. "I . . . didn't . . . I thought . . ."

"Josephine," Moriel said with deep sorrow, "this isn't you. What are you doing with this monster?"

At these words, the widow gathered herself and stiffened. "As if *you* should be judging anyone a monster. You don't know me as well as you think you do." If before that moment compassion remained within her, it either evaporated completely or burrowed too deeply to be recovered. Any evidence of remorse or inner conflict was replaced by cold determination.

"Now, really, Moriel, do I look like a monster?" Asmodeus smiled. His elegance certainly belied the evil within.

"You are Maweth, the Shadow Assassin," Mack boldly declared. "That's monstrous enough for me."

"The *Shadow Assassin*? Me? Now that is amusing. You Abidanians will believe anything. Although I must admit taking on the boogeyman identity certainly did help forward my plans."

"And what exactly are those plans?" Chaz Myrtle asked.

"To rule, of course. To rule in the name of Uriel, the rightful king of Mortania and to snuff out all memory of and allegiance to Abidan and its peasant king. I have long agreed with Uriel that the dignity of a ruler rests in his superiority over the rabble. A king of the people is unworthy of his throne."

Hearing the exchange echo through the tunnels of Mount Sar, the company of Abidanian knights quickened their pace toward the sound and approached the entrances with caution. Asmodeus relished in playing with his victims and loved to hear himself talk. Moriel used the time to slyly signal his troops.

"Now, where was I?" Asmodeus said. "Oh yes! I was answering Mr. Slade's question. It really isn't a bomb, although it could be used as one—a very powerful one in fact. It simply needs an identical epithymite stone set in place to complete the circuit and KABOOM!" Asmodeus flayed out his fingers in a dramatic flourish.

"But," he went on, "it can also be used as an impressively beautiful execution device, very effective at controlling miners when the fire gems fail to keep them in line. The effects of epithymite on a person's will isn't fail-safe. But, when coupled with *fear* . . . well, let's just say we've gotten a lot of work done in a very short period of time."

"Is this how you've thanked them for their work now that you are done with them?" Moriel chided.

"Done with them? Oh! You're wondering where all our miners are? The mine is closed today. Our workers are all safely locked in their cells in the mountain. You see, I knew you'd be joining us, and I wanted you to feel safe to explore." Moriel's stomach lurched realizing that Asmodeus had expected them. "It was a clever ruse, sending that big Fenek fellow to ask me for work. But I know Bruce Malvo. He could always use a big, strapping brute for something. And yet he pawned the man off on me. I thought that a bit unusual to begin with.

"But, to your question, no, I could not possibly dispatch five hundred mine workers in a single day. Let me show you how it works." Asmodeus walked over to the structure. "Sir Moriel unfortunately discovered that the interaction between the sage-stone and epithymite makes the apparatus impossible to disman-tle. He won't be using that hand for some time, I'm afraid. One can hardly approach the structure without a dangerous energy discharge. But, if one who wears my heart gem around his neck stands right here . . ." The villain stepped carefully into the space that closed the circuit of fire gems. "Well, then . . ."

"Then, he will be vaporized," Josephine stated bluntly, and ripping her own heart gem from around her neck, she tossed it over to Asmodeus.

Reflexively, Asmodeus caught the gem. Just at the moment he realized his grave error, a shocking effusion of light, heat, and smoke whisked him away into nothing but ash. Josephine's heart pendant fell to the ground with a *plink!* and bounced out of the device. The immediacy of Asmodeus's demise horrified the witnesses, leaving many sick at heart, despite their disdain for the former judge of Mortinburg.

Mack quipped, "Anyone want to argue about whether that's a death stone *now*?"

With a wicked smile, Josephine approached the sagestone device. "Finally! Thank you, Moriel. You have no idea how long I have been wanting to do that. He could be such a bore, don't you all think?"

For a lingering moment, no one knew what to do or think. Moriel reached out to Mrs. Pruitt, but she held up her hand saying, "Uh-uh . . . not so fast." Above her head she waved the final stone—the perfect match that would complete the fire gem circuit and detonate the structure. "I have worked too hard for this, Moriel. You are not going to stop me now."

Waljan was incredulous. "*You're* responsible for this, Mrs. Pruitt?"

Moriel shook his head gently and said with calm reason, "No, Josephine. You are not the type to take your pain out on the world. Revenge is a lonely business."

"And I am a lonely woman, Moriel, despite my 'type.' In fact, maybe because of my type. Asmodeus was a blind, small-minded fool. As if ruling a broken, suffering world could offer anything of value. No, ruling the world won't alleviate my pain. Destroying it will. The world is not worth ruling or saving. It is all just suffering."

"It isn't all suffering," Moriel insisted. "You can't know pain without also knowing joy. You suffer because you have loved. Embrace the love, Josephine. Don't dwell on the suffering," Moriel urged.

Tyre pushed through a group of knights who had been quietly edging their way into the chamber. "Mother?" Tyre said with intense compassion.

"Get him out of here—now!" Josephine screamed hysterically, threatening to place the final stone in the circuit. Moriel nodded to the knights nearest Tyre, and they tried to remove him but he slipped out of their grip and cried out, "I am not leaving, Mother!"

"All the more painful for you, then," she replied.

Moriel realized he must maintain calming reason and empathy. With his hands in a position of surrender, he indicated to all in the room that the situation was delicate. "You see? Even now you're a mother first. You don't have to do this, Josephine."

"It's a little late for that, don't you think?" Josephine spewed. "About twenty years too late."

"What is she talking about, Moriel?" Waljan asked.

Josephine laughed. "He doesn't even know the truth about Maweth, does he?"

"Josephine. Don't. You need to understand," Moriel pleaded.

"How does it feel, Moriel, now that I have the power over those *you* love?"

"It was a long time ago. Don't throw away your future over the past!"

"It was NOT a long time ago. Time stopped the day I lost him. And I have relived it every day since. It was yesterday. And this morning. And this very moment!" Tears streamed down Josephine's face and her body shook. Turning to Waljan she said, "The best place for a villain to hide is the last place you'd look for one. If you want to know who the Shadow Assassin is, ask the man who murdered my husband." Josephine stood, pointing at Moriel, with a conviction and pride that could not be shaken.

Waljan looked at Moriel, his eyes pleading for a denial. "What is she talking about?"

Dejected, tired, and struggling in pain, Moriel leaned against the cave wall more like a battered prisoner than the hero and mentor he'd been. "Wally, it was a long time ago. . . ."

"No . . . not you. That's impossible," Waljan lamented.

"I was a different man before I knew the king, Wally. . . ."

"You lied to me! I told you Maweth was Abidanian and you mocked me. Superstition, you said. Fantasy. You fought me. You sent me away! Do you have any idea what I have been going through? Because of you I couldn't say goodbye to Haden. And you expect me to *trust* you now?"

"Waljan, think about—"

"NO! This is all your fault!" Waljan seethed. Josephine regained her composure and began to enjoy the effect of her words. "People have suffered and died over this. You could have told me. *You* could have trusted *me*. We would have been able to stop this sooner."

"Waljan, calm down! In the name of the king!" Moriel commanded.

It was the last straw. Waljan drew his blade and lunged at Moriel with ferocity. Suddenly a sharp pain nipped at his hand, and Bergdis flew out of his grip and crashed to the floor. Penelope Longbow appeared from the dark recesses of the cavern, bow drawn and aimed at Waljan. Josephine watched with intense interest, while the knights, in utter confusion, couldn't decide where to point their blades.

"Stand down! Everyone!" Moriel demanded. Reluctantly, they obeyed.

"Peep?" Waljan said shocked and distraught. "Why?"

"Why? You're not thinking clearly, Waljan. I can't let you destroy yourself like this and take Moriel with you."

"He is Maweth. He's been lying to everyone. And *you* are pointing your arrow at *me*?"

Penelope lowered her weapon. "We are all Maweth, Waljan. Don't you see that? If you want to kill the Shadow Assassin, first kill the one that lives in your own heart."

"In *my* heart? After all these years, you don't know my heart, Penelope? I have always been there for you, for Haden, for the community. And rather than hold me up you tear me down. You just couldn't stand being second best, could you."

"Wally. This is not about being second best. . . ."

"No. It's about jealousy. It's about unseating the Hero of Mortinburg."

The words stung, not because they were untrue but because they were laced with truth. Penelope *had* been jealous of Waljan. But at this moment she was desperately trying to hold her world together without losing him. She failed to form words, but just shook her head.

Infuriated, Waljan ran from the chamber, leaving Bergdis on the floor where it had fallen.

"There is nowhere for him to run," Josephine laughed, but her words halted when Penelope aimed the point of her arrow in Josephine's direction with a look of fierce disdain. Josephine moved closer to the apparatus, threatening to detonate the sagestone. "If I die, you all die. But it hardly matters now."

"Of course it matters, Josephine," Moriel said quickly and gently. "Punish me if you must. I am nothing. But why punish the innocent?"

"*I'm* the innocent! I was punished. Why should others thrive when I am denied every happiness? Why shouldn't we all suffer equally? It isn't fair! You took my husband. Then you and your little minion, Waljan, took my son Caddock. After all I did for Wally! And that wasn't enough for you Abidanians. Then you had to take my son, Tyre. It's too much. Too much! Whoever this king really is, he must be the vilest of all kings to inspire so much devastation. Well, I can cause pain, too, if that's his game."

As the beleaguered widow carried on, overcome with sobs, Moriel placed his speaking stone on the ground in front of him and motioned for the knights to do the same. They surrounded the sagestone shards with speaking stones and watched with relief as the maddening hum of volatility died away.

"What's happening? What are you doing?" Josephine fretted. Several knights approached the platform and began to bat the fire gems away with their blades. "Stop!"

"It's over, Josephine," Moriel said with a relieved sigh. "The sagestone has been neutralized."

"Oh, it's hardly over," Mrs. Pruitt fumed. "You think I was relying on this device alone to accomplish my goals? You may have saved yourselves and you may have saved Mortania, but you have not saved the Realm. Thanks to the generosity of the Mortinburg Women's League, miniature versions of this device have been installed in mist chambers throughout Mortania. At their Mist Rite gatherings this evening, Abidanians, completely unaware of the fire gems they carry or wear, will detonate the sagestone. If it all goes by plan, they will destroy not only their chambers but all belief in the king and his Realm. You can send these knights running in all directions and they will not get back to their communities in time to stop it."

Moriel fell to his knees. He was completely out of options and resigned to whatever fate befell him. Suddenly, the speaking stone at his feet began to glow, faintly at first and then ever brighter, along with every stone that lined the room.

"He did it! Chen restored the Stone of Sages!" Peep announced gleefully.

The soft blue light spread out like a milky cloud. A chorus of sublime voices arose from the light followed by a host of Abidanian sages: Nava, the Servant-Heart, the Agasti of Miqodesh, Bindar the Beloved, and Dagmara of the Hills, among many others. Behind them stood several figures the knights recognized from their own lives, as well as Bartholomew Pruitt.

With compassion, Bartholomew looked toward Moriel, slumped in relief and too overwhelmed to notice his old friend. Then, Bart turned his attention to his family. "Come back to me!" he said, holding his hand out to Josephine.

"Bartholomew?" Josephine whimpered. "You're alive?"

"Of course I am, my darling. Why did you have any doubt?"

"But you died at the hands of Maweth! I saw it happen. . . . I buried you."

"Yes. So much horror and pain. But in that pain you've failed to see the truth, my love. Maweth also died that day. And in his place Moriel was born. You have nursed resentment against a man who repented of his crimes long ago and now serves the king with devotion. I'm at peace in the Realm and waiting for you. But the way you've chosen won't lead you home. The Sages of the Realm have notified the elders of your plans. You've failed. Let this hatred go. Come back to me. Come back to the king."

"No! This can't be. This is a trick!" Josephine insisted.

"There is so much to this world that we can't understand while we're still in it. Life on this side of the Wall limits us more than we can know. If you require a clear understanding of Truth before you can accept it, you will shut out the Truth that leads to clear understanding. Acceptance comes first, Josephine. I have been trying to reach you, but you refuse to hear. You shut me out the day you turned away from the king."

"Dad?" Tyre called.

"Tyre, my boy!" Bartholomew replied. "What a fine man you have become."

"It *was* you! I knew it. You gave this pouch to Wally."

"Yes. He is going to need you, son. He's suffering terribly."

"Is Caddock there with you?" Tyre asked his father.

"I can't answer that question. Take care of your mother. I must go now, but don't hesitate to use the stone, I will hear you."

"No one will hear you, Tyre!" Josephine scolded. "Can't you see this is a trick? A lie. You are so gullible you will believe anything no matter how fantastic! That is not Bartholomew Pruitt. He's an imposter. I don't know how Moriel is pulling this off, but I will not allow him to mock me!"

Josephine darted into the space where Asmodeus had vanished, clutching her fire gem as Tyre screamed for his mother to stop. She stood there, eyes squeezed shut, wrapped up in herself, hoping against hope for her own demise. But nothing happened. She opened her eyes, forced to accept that they had indeed succeeded in neutralizing the device. Laid open, completely exposed to the pity, judgment, and scorn of all in the room, Josephine crumpled to the floor.

Penelope dropped her bow and approached Josephine. She gently pried the fire gem from Josephine's hand and threw it as far from her as possible. Then she wrapped her arms around the broken woman and rocked her gently as Mrs. Pruitt dissolved pathetically.

"It's going to be okay, ma'am. You are going to be okay, I promise."

23

A New Adventure

The day Penelope left Master Chenaniah and Ander Slade behind at the Sanctuary, snow began falling on Shroud Peak, covering the mountain until late spring. Only in spring would anyone return to the Sanctuary. With Ander Slade to assist him, the winter would pass easier than it might have for Master Chenaniah.

Still, the weather was bitter and relentless. In a fit of youthful energy and creative ingenuity, Ander set about each day to make some structural or functional improvement to the Sanctuary. He insulated the master's hut, built an underground heating system, and set traps for game.

"Ander, you are spoiling the master!" Chenaniah scolded, quietly delighting in the new comforts. "I will only allow it to provide you opportunities for service."

"I will never understand the Agasti's desire for suffering, Master Chenaniah," Ander replied.

"It is not a desire for suffering, my boy. It is a desire for the fruits of suffering. Suffering strengthens us. Unites us. Saves us. But, most of all, suffering teaches us the nature of true love. At my age, though, I think I have learned all I can from suffering," Chenaniah chuckled.

The first week of the new year, in midwinter, Ander found

Master Chenaniah kneeling lifeless before the Stone of Sages. Alone, Ander buried him, reading the Words of Departure from the Book of Rites and Ceremonies he found in the master's hut. Alone, Ander continued to improve the Sanctuary grounds. Alone, Ander maintained the Stone of Sages, in communion with the Realm and the Elders of Abidan.

To everyone's knowledge, no previous Agasti had assumed responsibility for the Stone at such a young age, or single-handedly. Certainly, no one who was not Agasti. Ander Slade wasn't even Abidanian. But he conducted himself with a level of respect and care worthy of one who was united with the king.

None of it surprised Penelope when she, Chaz Myrtle, and the Slade brothers finally returned to Miqodesh with eleven new Agasti, appointed from among the Abidanian communities of Mortania. Penelope had always said that Ander was a remarkable kid. But as she and her companions entered the Sanctuary, it wasn't a boy who welcomed them. Ander now rivaled his brothers physically—leaner and lankier but just as tall.

"Who are you, and what did you do with my brother?" Mack teased, grabbing Ander and pulling him into a powerful embrace. Fenek and Ike joined in.

Ander soaked in this expression of endearment that had been so rare in the past few years. Then he enveloped Penelope, nearly lifting her off her feet, and gave Chaz a manly handshake. Chaz introduced each of the eleven Agasti, including Sir Allred of Mortinburg and Sir Eban of Dead Springs, who he'd already met.

"But, why only eleven? I thought the sanctuary housed twelve Agasti," Ander said.

"I tried to tell them, kid, but they wouldn't listen," Mack explained. "We've got to hit the trail and get back to bounty hunting. And we can really use this new physique of yours!" Mack beamed with pride for his not-so-little brother.

"I don't understand," said Ander.

Eban spoke for the elders. "My dear Mr. Slade, we see something in you uniquely suited to Agastic life. We were hoping that you would stay among us in the Sanctuary to learn the ways of Abidan and consider a future here.

"Well, of course I'll stay! Who's going to feed you all?" Ander laughed.

"Wait just a minute, kid!" Mack interjected. "Don't you think we should talk about this?"

"We will, Mack. I have so much to tell you about my six months here—what I have learned about the kingdom and about myself. Now, where is Sir Moriel and Waljan? I have been eager to see them."

A pall fell on the group and Mack grew noticeably agitated. No one knew how to tell Ander about what had happened on Mount Sar. He had heard about Asmodeus's defeat, the death stone, and how in the end they had freed the miners from their enslavement. Penelope tried to frame the rest as positively as she could.

"Wally has continued his Tribulation and we are not sure where he is. But he'll show up eventually. You know Wally!"

"And the other—I won't speak his name," Mack said, walking away. "I should start setting up our tents," he added over his shoulder.

Glowering as he watched Mack go, Eban explained, "Your brother has difficulty forgiving past wrongs. I understand, but it will not go well with him in the long run."

"Past wrongs? What could Moriel have done?" Ander asked.

"Apparently, your brother and Moriel had met before. Long ago, before Moriel was who he is now. Moriel's past remained in the past until 'the Shadow' was defeated on Mount Sar. This revelation has seriously compromised Moriel's effectiveness as a Knight of the Realm. He has lost the confidence of many and has been ordered to a period of solitude."

"Wow. That must be very hard for Moriel," Ander said.

Eban agreed. "It is hard for everyone. And forgiveness is a challenge for most."

In honor of Master Chenaniah, the new Agasti planned a

memorial and formal induction of the Stone of Sages. The Elders from each Mortanian town sent representatives to participate and pay their respects. Amid the tree blossoms that fell like tears, a procession solemnly strode to the gravesite. But the occasion was as was hopeful for a future reunion as it was sad for the master's parting.

After the ceremonies Ander and Penelope took a stroll through the campus. Eagerly, Ander showed off the practical improvements he made to the grounds—methods of purifying the well water, amending the garden soil, and storing smoked venison through the winter. Penelope was proud of her friend's ingenuity and commitment. But her periodic smiles faded too quickly, and her eyes wandered during long periods of silence as they walked. Ander knew her mind was elsewhere.

"You're worried about Wally, aren't you?" he asked.

"I'm worried about Wally. I'm sorry about Moriel. I miss the master terribly. And I am feeling very alone right now. Present company excepted, of course. But I will be leaving here soon, and I am pretty sure you are going to stay."

"What about Cully? You have him."

"Yes. I would be lost without him. As I think he would be without me. But that can't last. I need to make my own way and so does he."

"So, what is a Servant Heart to do without a heart to serve? You could always stay here. We could use a fierce security guard."

"Right." Penelope pushed him away, playfully. Then, seriously she added, "No. This servant's heart has to find Wally. And I'm not sure he wants to be found."

The brisk and salty west winds whipped up a foamy chop across the water. Waljan stood on the edge of the dock, looking east. He pulled a heavy cloak tighter around his shoulders against the chill of the early morning fog. Chiming a rhythmic ping, the rigging slapped against the hardware of a waiting tall ship. The gulls squealed plaintively.

The sound of thumping feet approached from behind. Waljan turned. "You came! I wasn't sure you would," he said.

Quadarius Quirinus Quaglio the Third gave Waljan a firm handshake and a pat on the shoulder. "How can I refuse such an offer?" he asked. "Although I thought I was accompanying a Knight of the Realm. You look more like a man in hiding."

"I'm sure you heard about the incident on Mount Sar last November," Waljan said.

"Bits. The highlights, I suppose. Nothing much about you, though." Quadarius replied.

"I guess I am easy to forget. In any case, I need a mission to reevaluate my choices. Searching for your father seemed a good place to start."

"Does this mean that you are leaving the Abidanian community? Abidan is a big part of who you are."

"That is part of the problem, Q. I don't know what about Waljan of the Realm is authentically me and what about me is authentically Abidanian. I can't know how I fit into the community until I know how I fit into the world. Everything went so fast. From moving to the city, to becoming the so-called Hero of Mortinburg. Most of it happened while I was still a boy. I almost feel like I was swept into it without making a conscious decision about it. I seem to be at war with myself all the time. Do you understand?"

"More than you could know," Quadarius replied. "You don't know how much this means to me. And where is Bo Dog? I expected he would come along."

"I left him in Miqodesh. I expect he is still there, but I don't know. I am sure someone is looking after him," Waljan said with a note of sadness. "No one knows that I contacted you? No one followed you here?"

"No. I had to tell Sir Eban something. I told him the truth; I am going on a sea voyage to find my father. He thought it would be good for me."

"Let's hope it's good for both of you," said Waljan.

"Let's hope it's good for all three of us," Quadarius replied.

From the crow's nest of the ship, a grungy sailor called for all to board. Waljan and Quadarius shouldered their packs and headed to the boarding plank in a line of men, a few women, and fewer children. The ship was one of the most magnificent things Waljan had ever seen. Man's ingenuity captivated him—the ability to imagine and then craft a vessel of interdependent components, each formed to specific purpose and working together, to carry people and cargo across vast planes of water by force of wind.

Having no money for the trip, Waljan and Quadarius sought out the quartermaster to report for duty. They would not be part of the regular crew but available for the most menial jobs that the crew needed done. It would be a challenge, but one the two men were ready to face.

As the marine layer lifted and the early summer sun glinted off the gentle ocean swells, the chief mate announced departure. Waljan and Quadarius received their orders and quickly delivered their packs to their assigned hammocks belowdecks. The ship shoved off. Snapping to full sail, it headed north out of North Bay and toward the great expanse of ocean. A new adventure had begun.